A QUESTION OF TRUST

•

Nina Coombs Pykare

AVALON BOOKS
THOMAS BOUREGY AND COMPANY, INC.
401 LAFAYETTE STREET
NEW YORK, NEW YORK 10003

© Copyright 1998 by Nina Coombs Pykare
Library of Congress Catalog Card Number 98-96611
ISBN 0-8034-9322-3
All rights reserved.
All the characters in this book are fictitious,
and any resemblance to actual persons,
living or dead, is purely coincidental.

PRINTED IN THE UNITED STATES OF AMERICA
ON ACID-FREE PAPER
BY HADDON CRAFTSMEN, BLOOMSBURG, PENNSYLVANIA

Chapter One

"I should never have worn these heels," Terry Matthews muttered to herself, picking her way around piles of dirt and through a treacherous patch of gravel. But the shoes—smart black pumps with medium heels—were standard wear for the kind of business meeting she'd just left. And when she was driving right by the job, there was no sense going home to change clothes first.

She ran a hand through hair the same color as the pumps and sighed. Sometimes she wondered if these bigger jobs were really worth the effort they took. When she'd started Matthews Concrete, on the proverbial shoestring, with determination and faith as her main assets, it'd been the little jobs that mattered—a driveway, a basement, a set of

2   *Nina Coombs Pykare*

outside steps. She'd prayed for jobs, and she was getting them.

She paused and looked at the piles of material for the new municipal office building. Now *this* job had come along. It was certainly a plum, a visible sign that Matthews Concrete was successful. She stood there for a moment, the late spring sun warm on her upturned face, the smell of wet concrete in her nostrils. And she smiled. This was her life—the one meant for her—and she loved it.

Then her smile faded. That rumor Pete had mentioned had been preying on her mind. If someone on City Council was really getting kickbacks . . . say Ben Toohey, for instance . . . He seemed the most likely. Of course, that was unfair, to suspect a man just because he'd been a thorn in her side ever since his election. Just because he was a pain didn't necessarily mean he was crooked. And rumors weren't always true.

Please, I hope there's no truth in this one. But there wasn't any point in worrying about it now. Just because this was the biggest job her company had ever undertaken didn't mean she had to get paranoid about the thing. She knew to have faith. Have faith and work hard, that's what Dad always said. And that's what he always did, too.

She willed the frown lines out of her forehead. Dad was right. Trust, that's what she needed. Trust that things would work out all right, if you did

A Question of Trust 3

your best. She'd done it with the small jobs. She'd do it with this one. Only sometimes, when she got scared, she forgot that trust.

Well, right now she'd better go talk to Pete. After all, that *was* why she'd stopped at the site, to give him the latest word about the Carson job. Then she had to get back to the office. Matthews Concrete had other jobs besides this one. Thank goodness.

And if there was graft . . . well, she wouldn't be any part of a thing like that. Truth was, she wouldn't even have bid on this job if she'd known about the rumors then.

She stopped, swallowing a groan. Who was that standing beside Pete? He sure didn't belong here, that tall, lean man whose yellow hard hat was in sharp contrast to his expensive business suit. Probably another snooper from City Council, though she didn't recognize him from behind. They liked to come around, acting important and asking stupid questions that showed how little they knew about concrete construction.

She really resented the Council's interference. She was good at her work, and she knew it. If they didn't trust her to do the job right, they shouldn't have accepted her bid.

Swinging her hard hat from her index finger, she squared her shoulders. Might as well get it over with. Let the snooper ask his questions and get out of there. Then they could all get back to work.

The men stood with their backs to her, facing the new building site. The stranger was tall, probably over six feet. Taller than Pete, and Pete was no shorty. The stranger had broad shoulders, too, and dark brown hair that curled from under his hard hat.

Ouch! Served her right for not watching where she was going. A sharp pebble must have worked its way into her pump and was stabbing her foot. Better get it out now, before she got a blister. She leaned against a convenient pile of concrete blocks.

She was standing there, her pump in her hand, when Pete's voice floated to her through the babble of construction noise. "Been with her four years now. Best boss a man ever had."

She smiled. Pete was the best foreman in the world, too. She stooped to put on her shoe, but froze halfway when the stranger said, "Maybe so. But I still say this is no business for a woman."

Her pump hit the ground and she jammed her foot into it, the leftover anger from this morning's Council meeting boiling to the surface. Another pompous know-it-all. Probably couldn't tell a trowel from a bull float. And he was going to question *her*.

Anger wasn't a good thing to feel, but the men

A Question of Trust 5

she'd just left had nearly driven her to distraction with their questions. They didn't know a thing about working concrete. But they sat there, squeezed into their expensive leather chairs, those awful smelly cigars clouding up the room, and asked their stupid questions. And even worse than that, worse than the endless questions, was her suspicion of them, her fear that one of them would come to her later to suggest graft. Well, she just wouldn't do it. She couldn't do it. She was the best concrete finisher around, the most honest, too. And that was the absolute truth.

She threw back her head and pulled in a good lung full of construction smells—crisp fresh lumber, sharp acrid steel, and the indescribable yet seductive odor of wet concrete. *This* was her world. And she loved it.

Might as well get on with it. She rounded a pile of gravel and came up to face them. "Hi, Pete."

The stranger had golden eyes, the color of sunlight on fallen leaves. And there was something about them. . . .

But she couldn't think about that now.

"Hi, Terry." Pete's gravelly voice carried puzzlement, maybe at seeing her on the site in such dressy clothes. "How'd the meeting go?"

She wrenched her gaze away from the stranger's. "Same old stuff."

The stranger's gaze hadn't left her. He was

calmly taking in everything from her smart business suit to the pumps. And his generous mouth curved in a smile. Well, she wasn't going to smile back. She wasn't. Let him take his charm somewhere else.

His smile widened and his golden eyes gleamed at her. "So you're Terry."

"I'm Terry Matthews." She made her voice crisp and businesslike.

"Of Matthews Concrete."

"Exactly."

He shook his head. "Really, Terry . . ."

"You may call me Miss Matthews." She could feel Pete looking at her. She was being silly. She didn't know anything about this man yet (well, except for his overheard remark and her suspicion that he was a Council snooper) but she'd let her annoyance with them carry over to him. That wasn't fair. But she didn't *want* to be fair. Well, she did want to be fair, but she was tired of dealing with the Council. Really tired.

"Miss Matthews," he began again, his eyes dancing with amusement. "I just don't understand what a woman like you—a very beautiful woman— is doing in work like this."

He needn't think he could get around her with compliments. Or by looking at her with such admiration.

A Question of Trust   7

"This is no business for a woman," he went on. "It's difficult and it's dirty."

At least he said it to her face. That was something. "I'm really sorry." Her tone could have etched the words in steel. "That you don't approve of me, Mr. . . ."

"Green. Harrison Green."

The name sounded familiar, but she couldn't place it. Pete coughed. "I don't believe it's any of your business what I do for a living," she went on. "I like my work, and I'm good at it."

Green's smile could have melted the steel pillar behind her. She almost turned to see if it had.

"I was merely saying that you're far too beautiful a woman to be wasting your life like this."

Wasting? How dare he be so patronizing! Who did he think he was? "I don't happen to feel that my life is wasted." Her voice was growing even sharper, but she didn't care. "And now, Mr. Green, if you'll excuse me, I have things to discuss with my foreman."

Pete coughed again. She gave him a worried look. Sounded like he was catching something. Maybe he ought to see a doctor.

Harrison Green laughed. "Sorry, Miss Matthews. I'm afraid you'll have to wait to talk to Pete. I have some things to discuss with you. Things about the job. You appear to have forgotten . . .

8 *Nina Coombs Pykare*

But I am the new city manager. So you're going to have to deal with me."

Of course! Now she remembered. Her cheeks grew warm. Pete must have been coughing to warn her. If she hadn't been so mad from this morning . . . "I see." The Council had wasted her whole morning with their useless questions and now this— She pulled in a calming breath. She would not lose her cool. She had taken this job, and she'd have to do her best with it.

"What is it you want to discuss?" she asked, trying to be more civil. But they could have sent this man, this obvious charmer, because she was a woman, to see if she would . . .

"Certain specifications . . ." he began.

Not specs again! They'd been over this so many times. She was sick of it. "The specifications are all in the plans," she said, forcing herself to hold on to her calm. "All agreed upon and all being followed. To the T."

He nodded, his expression sober. "And how many yards of concrete did you say the job will take?"

She tried to hold on to her temper, she really tried. "Mr. Green, that too is information you already have. I'm a businesswoman. My time is precious. I don't like to waste it giving you information you already have." Why couldn't he

A Question of Trust

9

just leave? Go back to the rest of them and let her get back to work.

She turned. "Pete."

"Yeah, Terry?" His craggy forehead was wrinkled in a frown. No wonder. He'd never seen her behave like this before. Customers could be irritating, but she always reminded herself that they should be treated with respect.

So why did Harrison Green bring out the worst in her? Why couldn't she give him the benefit of the doubt? Well, she didn't have time to figure it out now.

"Listen, Pete. I stopped by to tell you that we got the Carson job, too." She swallowed a sigh. Green hadn't taken her hint that he leave. He'd just stepped off to one side and was looking over the job. Or pretending to.

"Good." Pete tried a smile, a not very effective one. "I'll set it up for Friday." He lost the smile and frowned. "Ah, Terry, you all right? Something happen this morning?"

She shook her head. "Not really. Just the same old stupid stuff. The same old questions. So I answered them all again." She swallowed. "How long has this Green been hanging around?"

"Not long." Pete's eyes were anxious. "Seems like a nice enough guy. Except," he added, as her face darkened, "for his attitude about you and the business, of course."

"Of course," she repeated. Well, there was no getting around it. She'd have to deal with Green. He *was* the Council's representative. But she didn't have to trust him. On every job there were unpleasant things. That was part of life.

Pete was still peering at her anxiously. "Ah, Terry, you know, you aren't wearing your hard hat."

"Oh. Thanks, Pete." He was right. She always wore her hard hat on the job. One dropped tool could mean the end of a productive life. She'd been so riled up, though, that she'd forgotten all about it. The Council did that to her. And she shouldn't let them. *Take it easy,* she told herself. *I know I can get through this.*

She clapped the hard hat on her head. If only she'd gone back to the office first and changed into her other work clothes—the T-shirt, jeans, and heavy work shoes that she finished concrete in. She felt more like herself in them. "I'll take care of Mr. Green," she told Pete. "You can go back to work."

Pete hesitated, almost as though he didn't want to leave her alone with Green. Then he nodded and turned away, still frowning.

Chapter Two

Terry stood there for a moment, breathing in the construction smells, letting the construction sounds roll over her, calming herself with their familiarity. This was her world. If only Green would go away. But she wasn't going to be that blessed.

"So . . ." Green moved over beside her, blocking out the sun, making her feel small. And annoyed all over again. "Have you been in the business long?" he asked.

Well, she supposed he had a right to ask about her credentials. That *was* part of his job.

"I've had my own company for four years. Before that I worked as a finisher and before that as an apprentice, learning the trade. And I assure you, I *know* my trade."

"Why *this* trade?" he asked, raising an eyebrow. "I mean, it is a rather unusual trade for a woman."

She held on to her temper. It wasn't the first time she'd been asked that question. And she had her answer ready. "I like building things."

He waited. Obviously he wasn't going to be satisfied by such a brief answer.

"My father was in the construction business," she went on. "My uncle built houses. My father did the concrete work. My cousins helped. I helped, too." She laughed. "The boys told me girls couldn't do those things." She was silent for minute, staring over his shoulder, remembering.

"So you showed them they were wrong." His tone, soft and sympathetic, urged her on.

"Something like that. I build things," she repeated. "Things that last."

"You mean . . . you don't want children?"

Her gaze snapped back to him. He was looking at her strangely. "Of course I want children. What has *that* to do with *this?*"

He shrugged. "Well, it just seemed that you're so intent on the business. It's hard to see how you'd have time for a family." His golden eyes threatened to burn a hole through her head and out the back of her hard hat. "And what does your husband want? Doesn't he—"

"I have no husband. Yet." Now why had she

A Question of Trust
13

added that "yet"? She wasn't embarrassed by being unmarried. She'd been asked. And she'd said yes. But a week before the wedding Jeff had told her he'd found someone else, small delicate Jeannie Wilson, soft helpless Jeannie. And that had been the end of that.

It had hurt. It'd hurt a lot. But she knew it was for the best. Jeff definitely couldn't be trusted.

She looked Harrison Green straight in the eye. "I built my business with a lot of hard work. And sweat." She watched for the flicker of distaste in his expression, but it didn't come. "And I'm very good at it."

He nodded. "You must be proud of what you've achieved."

She stared at him in surprise. "Is this the man who said this was no business for a woman?"

His eyes darkened, like a cloud moving in front of the sun. Then he smiled and the sun came out again. "Yes, it is. Sorry I said that. I was surprised, that's all. You're a beautiful woman, and to be doing work like this . . . But I can see I was wrong. Will you accept my apology?"

What a smile the man had! She could feel herself thawing toward him. But she had to be careful. She didn't know anything about him. She couldn't afford to trust him. Not after the mess she'd made with Jeff, and with this graft thing hanging over her.

14　　　　*Nina Coombs Pykare*

She forced herself to be calm and cool. "Now, Mr. Green, I've really spent too much time here. I'm needed back at my office. I'm licensed. I'm bonded. Everything is in proper order. You have the plans, the specifications, and the contract. There's nothing else you need to know."

"One more thing," he said, lowering his voice.

Now it was coming. He was going to talk about graft. She braced herself. It had to be Toohey. But Green probably wouldn't tell her *who* had sent him.

"What time shall I pick you up for dinner?"

For a moment she gaped at him. The wash of relief was so overwhelming that she almost said yes. But she still didn't know anything about him. And she didn't get involved with men she couldn't trust. It was easier that way.

"I'm afraid I'm busy tonight," she said. "I have to wash my hair." *That was unkind. Not the way I usually behave.*

For a long moment Green's eyes burned into hers. She almost had to take a step backward to get away from his probing gaze.

A dropped tool hit the ground nearby and they both jumped. There was a real world out there. And work to do.

She looked over his left shoulder. No more staring into the man's eyes. "Good-bye, Mr. Green."

"*Au revoir,* Miss Matthews." He kept looking

A Question of Trust   15

at her until she turned away, heading back to the parking lot with as much dignity as she could muster.

The distance to the van seemed awfully long. She could feel him watching her as she skirted mounds of sand and gravel, detoured around stacks of lumber and steel pillars. When she was away from the building, she took off the hard hat and shook free her hair. Whether or not the man was in on the graft, he was dangerous to her peace of mind.

Half an hour later, she turned in the drive of the big old double house that served as both home and office. She smiled. The old place looked good. She'd made the right decision in buying it. She'd needed space to store rails and pins, wheelbarrows and bull floats, to say nothing of the other tools of the trade, and the truck that Pete sometimes drove.

She pulled the van around back to its usual spot. The house *was* big—for one woman. But it would be an ideal place to raise kids. Children should have a big house, a big yard. Space.

And a father. *Oh, no!* Why should she imagine a bunch of chattering laughing kids running to meet her? Kids who had *his* golden eyes. What silliness!

She shoved open the van door and stepped out into the sunshine. Harrison Green wasn't going to elbow his way into her personal life. It was going to be all business between them.

She hurried up the walk as fast as the pumps would allow. First she was going to get into her comfortable clothes. And second she was going to forget all about Harrison Green. Wipe him out of her memory like she troweled unwanted marks out of wet concrete.

She changed into her work clothes, smiling while she laced up her heavy shoes. If he saw her now—in her frayed and faded jeans, T-shirt speckled with concrete, and shoes that looked the worse for wear—Harrison Green wouldn't give her a second glance.

As Jeff had jokingly, or not so jokingly, put it, in her work clothes she looked like a Goodwill reject. But what Jeff had said didn't hurt anymore. She was over him. She could be herself now. She could even see it was a good thing she hadn't married a man like Jeff, a man who couldn't be trusted.

She settled behind her desk and picked up pencil and tablet. The new city manager wasn't going to be easy to deal with. Still, it was hard to imagine him taking graft. He didn't seem the sort to be a flunky. Maybe the rumor wasn't true. Maybe no one on the council had sticky fingers. She hoped they didn't. She prayed they didn't.

She chewed absently on her pencil, bits and

A Question of Trust   17

pieces of gossip flitting through her mind. Harrison Green was well-to-do, but she didn't need gossip to know that. The expensive suit—and the way he wore it—showed it. She knew he had no kids, but he'd had a wife—once. Terry didn't know what had happened to her, but he was single now. Why should such a man want to be city manager?

She pulled a tablet toward her. What Harrison Green did or didn't do was none of her business. Listening to her messages was. But before she could rewind the tape, she heard someone come up on the veranda. Company would be welcome. Anyone to take her mind off Green and his golden eyes.

The door opened. Oh, no! Him again. She scrambled to her feet.

"Nice office," Harrison Green said. "Very pleasant." He stepped in and closed the door.

"What do you want?"

"Business, of course."

"I thought we'd attended to all our business." *Just remember,* she told herself. *Business, all business.*

He shook his head. His hair was rich chocolate brown, with a curl that would make any woman envious.

"No, we didn't," he replied. "You were in such a rush earlier that I didn't get to finish." His smile was warm and friendly. Too warm. Too friendly.

"What we need is a nice quiet place. No interruptions. Then we can handle all this nicely."

Her thoughts tumbled about in her head. Did he want to take her to dinner to talk about graft? Or was he interested in her, her as a person? Well, what if he was? She wasn't interested in him. *Stick to business.* "Anything you have to say to me can be said here."

What was there about the man? It was almost like he could see things about her that she didn't know herself. Things she didn't *want* to know.

"No, we need to go to dinner." His smile didn't fade, but his voice was firm, determined.

"I told you . . ."

"Yes, I know." Was that a hint of laughter around his mouth? "You have to wash your hair." His gaze went to her hair. His smile was faintly amused. "I do think, though, that for the sake of your business, you could make a little sacrifice."

He took another step, leaned across the wide desk, and took a strand of her hair between his fingers. "Doesn't feel a bit dirty to me," he said. "Surely it can wait one more day."

For one moment she was paralyzed. Those golden eyes . . .

She drew back, her hair sliding free of his fingers. Her heart pounded in her throat and kept the words from coming out. All she could manage was a stammered "I . . ."

A Question of Trust   19

"I knew you'd see it my way. After all, this *is* business."

"But—" She began another protest, but he cut her off.

"I take it you live here, too. I'll be back to get you around seven."

His gaze slid to her clothes. "Wear something nice. We're going to the country club."

"But I . . ." Her protest rang in empty air. He was already gone, closing the door quietly behind him. There was time to jump up, to go after him and yell that she wasn't going anywhere with him. But she didn't move; she just sat there, listening to the sound of his footsteps dying away. What an infuriating man. And yet . . .

Chapter Three

Terry was ready before seven. Something told her Green wasn't the sort of man to be kept waiting. But if he was expecting someone sweet and feminine he was in for a shock. She'd been really tempted to greet him in her oldest and shabbiest work clothes. But second thought had convinced her that he was just the sort to smile smugly and start right off for the country club, regardless of what she was wearing. And she had no desire to make a fool of herself.

He needn't think, either, that she'd be awed by the country club. She'd been there more than once, but never with anyone like him. Someone who aggravated her so. *Sorry. I know I shouldn't judge people.*

A Question of Trust   21

She smoothed the long skirt of her royal blue dress. Bought for last Christmas Eve's ball, it was probably a little elaborate for a simple dinner like this. But at the country club it was better to be too well dressed, rather than not well enough. And in this gown—simple yet stylish—she could feel a match for Green. *Forgive me,* she breathed. *I don't know why the man annoys me so much.*

Instead of letting her hair hang loose on her shoulders or pulling it back in a ponytail as she usually did, she had coiled it into a smooth knot, held in place with glittering combs. Sapphires gleamed on her throat and dangled from her earlobes. She eyed herself in the mirror. Yes, if Harrison Green thought he was slumming, he was going to have another thing coming. She could hold her own with any man—or woman.

When the doorbell rang, she jumped, startled by the sound even though she was expecting it. Her silver sandals whispered softly on the carpet as she hurried across the room. She wished they had higher heels—she didn't like the way Green towered over her. But anything higher would make her feet hurt, and the evening was going to be difficult enough.

She pulled in a deep calming breath, counted to ten, and opened the door. He stood there in a white tux—the best-looking man she'd ever seen. And it was a good thing she'd taken that breath because now, looking at him, it was really hard to breathe.

His smile made him look like a different man. Even more handsome. "Wow!" he said. "Is that really you?"

She smiled. There was no way she could stop herself. "Yes, it's really me. Good evening, Mr. Green. I'll be right with you."

He shook his head as though to clear it and his lips curved into a mischievous grin. "I didn't know I was having dinner with the Dragon Lady."

What kind of line was that? "If you'd like to step in, I'll just get my wrap, and we can be on our way."

He stepped in, his gaze taking in her rose and white living room. "Got a club in here?"

She was startled into asking, "A club? What on earth do you want with a club?"

"Why, to beat off the men, of course." His eyes twinkled. "The Dragon Lady's very beautiful, you know."

She kept her reply light. "And deadly, don't forget. I read *Terry and the Pirates,* too."

His smile warmed her. "I'm glad I'm having dinner with *this* Terry and not the other one." For a long moment he stood, his gaze holding hers captive.

Enough, she told herself. *Remember, this is a business dinner.* But under the long gown her

A Question of Trust   23

knees weakened and her heart pounded so hard she was sure he must be able to see it jumping around in her chest.

He took a step toward her, those golden eyes so compelling, burning into hers. Another step and still she stood, mesmerized. He stopped only inches away. "You're beautiful," he whispered softly. "A more beautiful woman was never made."

His hand slid under her chin, tilting it up. For a long moment his eyes held hers. *No,* she told herself. *He's too dangerous.* She pulled away, evading his kiss, and picked up her shawl with trembling fingers. "Shall we go? I hope there's something good on the menu tonight. I'm starving."

Her voice was too bright and it had quavered slightly in the middle of her speech, but at least she had avoided that kiss.

She wasn't sure why that should be important. She didn't kiss on the first date, of course. She didn't kiss a man unless she thought she loved him. But Harrison Green was different. There was something compelling about him, as though he had the power to make her feel and act in ways she never had before. And that was dangerous. Good grief! She still hardly knew anything about the man. And she couldn't forget his connection to the City Council—whatever it was. She didn't dare

24   *Nina Coombs Pykare*

forget it. That was the only thing she really knew
about him—that the Council had hired him and he
could be connected to graft. She threw the light
shawl over her shoulders, and picked up her purse.
"Let's go, Mr. Green."

Not looking at his face, she hoped to make the
moment pass, but the grip of his fingers on her
elbow as they descended the porch steps was just
a little too tight.

Tight enough to tell her he didn't like being
thwarted. Well, tough luck, he'd have to live with
it. She didn't like the way he was treating her,
like— She realized suddenly that she wasn't sure
what he was treating her like. On the surface it
was all socially acceptable—part of the game people played. But underneath there was that something else. She felt it even though she couldn't give
it a name. And it scared her.

"Did you read the old *Terry and the Pirates*?"
he asked, guiding his long black Mercedes out
onto the road. "Or the new strips coming out
now?"

"The old ones," she said. "My mother had a
lot of old comic books. She kept them from when
she was young. I was an only child and didn't
always have someone to play with. So I used to
read them on rainy days."

He nodded. She risked a glance at his profile.
He was handsome, all right, in that rugged, been-

A Question of Trust 25

around way. And definitely dangerous to a woman like her. Any woman, probably.

He half-turned, meeting her gaze. "What's your real name?"

"Theresa."

"And your mother's?"

Now what was he getting at? "Theresa. I was named after her."

"I see."

Why that tone in his voice? Probably she shouldn't ask, but she did. "You see what?"

He gave her a long look, so long she almost reminded him to watch the road. "It's simple," he went on. "Instead of identifying with the women characters, your mother identified with Terry. She became the hero. And she encouraged you to do the same. *That's* why you took on a man's job."

She laughed out loud. Of all the farfetched . . . He was certainly going to a lot of trouble to explain a very simple thing. "And when did you get your degree in psychiatry, Doctor? I work with concrete because I *like* it. It's as simple as that."

He shrugged. "Maybe."

He sounded like he wasn't convinced. Well, neither was she. Let him keep his silly theories. She knew better.

"So." He glanced her way again. "Do you live in that big house alone?"

"At the moment." He sure asked a lot of questions.

He raised an eyebrow. "It seems awfully big for a woman alone."

Now why was she aggravated? *Give me patience.* She kept her voice calm. "Maybe. But I don't intend to be alone forever."

"I'm glad." The softness in his voice took her by surprise. "I can see the place full of kids," he went on. "Kids with your coal-black hair and green eyes."

She tried to laugh, to ease the tension she was feeling, but her laughter didn't ring true. She just hoped *he* couldn't tell. "It's not very likely that they'd *all* look like me."

"No, that's true." He sounded thoughtful. "Probably some of them would look like your husband."

"Probably." She wanted to make her tone light and laughing, but the picture that came into her mind, the picture of children who looked like him, was too vivid. *What's wrong with me? I shouldn't be thinking things like this. I just met the man and now I'm thinking about children? That's not like me.*

She turned a little more to look fully at him. "You . . . you have no children?"

"No." His tone was so bitter she actually winced. "My ex-wife had no use for them."

A Question of Trust   27

"No use?" What an odd thing to say. "For children?"

"Right." The bitterness grew sharper. "A strange way to talk about children, isn't it? But those are her exact words. I'm not likely to forget them." His face twisted in pain. "She had a *career*. And that was what was important to her." His emphasis made the word cut. "And nothing must stand in the way of that. Nothing. That's why she left me."

How awful to be denied the right to a family. What kind of woman had the man married? "I'm sorry." She murmured the words almost without thinking.

"Don't be." His words were crisp. "It's better this way. She can have her career. And I can have what I want—a home and family. With a woman who loves me more than her career."

There they were again in her mind—the children with the golden eyes. Only now they didn't come alone to meet her. . . . *He* was there, too, smiling with open arms.

That's stupid, she told herself sharply. *He wants someone to be there waiting when he comes home. Not the other way around.* A sigh escaped her.

His right hand left the steering wheel and settled over her left, its warmth comforting. "No need to feel sad for me. I'm going to have what I want. That's the sort of man I am."

There was something about his voice, something that touched her heart, so that for one breathless moment *she* wanted to be the woman who waited for him, wanted to share her life with him. Then sanity returned. Though the picture in her mind was pretty, it didn't show what would really happen. Her business was part of her life. She wouldn't—she couldn't—give it up. Not without anger and the deepest sort of pain. And the resentment over that would spoil any marriage with the man who caused it.

Carefully she withdrew her fingers from his. "Mr. Green . . ."

"Come on now." His gaze met hers, those golden eyes so warm and friendly she wanted to melt. "This is unfair treatment." He grinned. "You're discriminating against me because I'm a man. You know that if *you* were a man, we'd be on a first-name basis. You saw how Pete and I hit it off right away."

His tone was so rueful that she had to laugh. And unfortunately, what he said was true. In fact, if he were any other man, she'd have been calling him by his first name right away. "Oh, all right. I'll call you Harrison."

"Good, Terry." There was something about the way he said her name, something that warmed her deep inside in spite of all her efforts not to let it.

A Question of Trust 29

"That's more like it." He pulled up to the country club door. "And now for that dinner."

She hesitated as the admiring parking lot valet whisked the car off, but finally she put her hand on the arm Harrison offered her. She didn't want to touch him. And yet . . . she wanted to walk right into his arms. To have the kiss she had denied herself earlier. Good grief! She'd never thought such things about a man before. Harrison Green set off strange, ambivalent feelings in her. Attracting while he repelled. And she wasn't quite sure how to handle that. But she did have to handle it, especially since she couldn't be sure what it was he really wanted from her, since she had to remember that he might be part of the graft.

Help me with this, please, she prayed. *Help me to do my job. And help me not to be carried away by Harrison Green.*

Chapter Four

Harrison let her look over the menu for several minutes before he asked, "See anything that appeals to you?"

"Ah . . . I can't make up my mind." Terry certainly wasn't going to admit that she hadn't read a word she was staring at. She forced herself to concentrate. "Ah, let's see. I guess I'll have the sole almondine. Rice pilaf. Celery-seed dressing on the salad."

He nodded. "An excellent choice." He gave the waiter a brilliant smile. "I'll have the same."

Did he do that on purpose, order the same meal to make me feel closer to him? Still, I liked it, I liked the way it made me feel. I've got to be careful. Please, please, help me.

A Question of Trust   31

Harrison was in the wrong business. With that smile, that charm, he ought to be a salesman—or a politician. She got an instant picture of him kissing a long line of babies, smiling warmly at each one. It made her chuckle.

"What's so funny?" he asked, the little laugh lines crinkling around his eyes.

"I was thinking what a good politician you'd make. I could actually see you kissing babies." *And their mothers would be sure to vote for you.* But she didn't say that.

He smiled, displaying even white teeth. "I thought about it when *I* was a boy. When I was intrigued by how cities are run."

"A funny thing for a kid to be interested in." Strange, she was saying just what she was thinking. She hadn't done that for a long time. Since Jeff, she hadn't been this open with any man.

Harrison leaned toward her, giving her all his attention. "Yes, I suppose so. The whole thing started on Government Day. When I was elected mayor."

With all the girls' votes. She tried to imagine a young Harrison Green. He must have been a real heartbreaker.

"I got to spend the day with the mayor," he went on. "I felt real big." He rolled his eyes. "Sat at his desk, watched him sign papers, went to the

Council meeting. Afterward, I swamped Dad with all kinds of questions.''

His little chuckle invited her to share his amusement. ''I guess Dad didn't think much of politicians either. He told me about city managers and how, since they were outside of politics and more objective about things, they could do a better job than elected officials. I liked the idea. So I studied government in school, and administration in college, got some experience.'' He shrugged. ''And here I am.''

''I heard you came here from a big city.'' *Talk to him,* she told herself. *Don't think about how he makes you feel.*

His eyes went cloudy. ''Carol liked cities. After she left me . . .''

He shrugged, his shoulders stretching his dinner jacket taut. Why did he have to be so attractive? Why couldn't he be somebody ordinary?

''I never cared that much,'' he went on. ''Cities were her kind of place. And I wanted a change. New faces. New friends. You know.'' His voice softened on the last word and she felt an answering softness deep inside her.

''I liked the sound of Stonybrook. I like living in the country. And it's not all that far from Cleveland if I want cultural stimulation.''

She nodded, swallowing an urge to giggle. What

A Question of Trust   33

was there about the man that made her feel so good? Made her want to laugh out loud?

Their salads arrived and she turned to hers with relief, pausing after a few bites to remind him, "I believe you said you had business to discuss with me?"

He nodded, his expression somber, though his eyes gleamed with something. Mischief, maybe? He patted his breast pocket. "In fact, I have my list of questions right here."

She heaved a sigh of resignation. "I hope they make more sense than the ones you asked earlier. Or the ones the Council's always throwing at me."

"Oh, they do." His eyes were so bright. Was he laughing at her? "I've had more time to think about them."

He *was* laughing. "All right, ask away." *Please let these questions really be about concrete, not about my getting on the take.*

He looked down at the list. "Why are you making certain areas of floor five inches thick instead of the usual four?"

She let her breath out slowly. So far, so good. "Ned Fisher, the architect, felt that those areas would undergo more strain. Everyone bid on the same specs, you know."

"I know." Harrison's dark brows drew together in a frown. "I'm not looking for discrepancies, Terry. I just want to understand what's going on.

I want to do my job. Doing it well is important to me.''

She could believe that, but . . .

''I hope you aren't thinking of me as an enemy.'' His eyes darkened and his hand stole across the table and captured hers. She felt a kind of contentment stealing over her. ''I want us to be friends,'' he said. But the way he said it and the pressure of his fingers on hers made her feel like they'd *been* friends, more than friends, forever.

She looked into his eyes, like swimming through golden pools of sunlight. *Get a grip,* she told herself. ''The cement business isn't difficult to understand,'' she told him. ''It's all very sensible.'' Not like what she was feeling about him. Not at all.

''I'm sure it is.''

She clenched the napkin in her lap. She wasn't going to reach out and touch him. She wasn't.

''I'm glad to hear it.'' He smiled. ''Because in some areas . . . you don't appear to be sensible at all.''

Now what was he talking about? ''I don't think you know enough about me to make any judgments.''

''You're right,'' he replied, his eyes lighting with triumph. Too late she saw that she had fallen into a trap that had been subtly baited. ''I *don't* know you very well.'' He squeezed her fingers

A Question of Trust 35

again, fingers that he still held. "But that's a situation I want to remedy. As soon as I can."

She pulled her hand away, returning to her meal. But her thoughts were a mad whirl. It looked like what he had in mind didn't have a thing to do with concrete! But she couldn't afford to care for a man she hardly knew, no matter how much he attracted her. And how could she care for a man she had doubts about?

"I'm afraid I'm a very private person," she began, but her voice faded under the look in those eyes.

"And I'm a very persistent one." His implacable expression was almost frightening. A shiver went over her. If he wanted to know something, he would discover it. And if he was connected to the graft? But she couldn't think about that now.

She tried a little laugh. "The job, remember the job?"

He smiled and returned to his salad, but she knew he hadn't changed his mind. He was not only persistent, he was downright stubborn. But he'd met his match. She wasn't going to tell him anything she didn't want to.

He finished his salad before he spoke again. "How's the drainage on the land?" he asked while the waiter removed their plates and brought them the main course.

Good, he was back to business. "Fisher decided

where to put the building," she said. "But it looks good to me. We put in plenty of drainage tile. I don't foresee any problems."

She paused. She didn't want to play anymore. This game was getting tiresome. "You know, Green, this thing is pretty transparent."

"What thing?" His face was all innocence, but his eyes gleamed with mischief again.

"This 'teach me about concrete' thing." She forced herself not to drop her gaze from the intensity in his, to keep the contact between them. "I like to talk shop as well as the next man." There was something not quite right about that, but she didn't stop to analyze it. "But this is silly. And so are your questions."

He couldn't even manage to look properly sheepish, not with that expression of triumph on his face. "At last! I wondered how long I'd have to keep this up. Now we can get down to the real business of the evening."

"Which is—" She bit back the rest of the question. He was too quick on the uptake. Everything she said played into his hands.

"Which is getting to know each other, of course. Much more fascinating than concrete." His smile was so charming that several passing women turned to look back over their shoulders at him— with obvious appreciation.

But she was immune to charming smiles.

A Question of Trust   37

Wasn't she? "And what if I don't want to know you better? What if I know quite enough about you now?" She kept her tone light and teasing, but his golden eyes darkened.

"You're being unfair again," he complained. "Here I am, a newcomer in your town. And all alone. The least you could do is offer me a little friendliness."

She couldn't help laughing at his woebegone expression. Harrison Green wouldn't be alone for long. That was one thing she could be sure of. In fact, from the looks they were sending his way, the women at the next table would have been glad to remedy that situation right now. But she didn't bother to give *him* that information. His head was big enough as it was.

She pulled her mouth into soberness. "How do you expect me to offer friendliness to a man who insulted me before he even met me?"

"Who, me?" He couldn't quite make his expression sober.

She shook her head. "That innocent act won't work with me. I heard you tell Pete that concrete was no business for a woman. And then you told me, right to my face."

His smile was devastating. It could have made her forgive him almost anything.

"I told you I didn't mean that. Really. It's just that a beautiful woman like you . . ." His voice deepened and softened, drawing her into closer intimacy. "You shouldn't have to worry about bills and estimates, or go grubbing around in concrete. You should be cherished and protected, surrounded by beautiful things."

So that was it. She stiffened and pulled back the fingers he had captured again. "You forget . . ." The words came slowly, because a little part of her was still held by the tenderness in his voice. ". . . I *like* grubbing around, as you call it. I like worrying about bills and estimates. I'm *alive*, you see." Her voice gained strength. "I'm not a thing. Not a rare piece of art to be protected and cherished. I'm a *person*, with a person's need to do things, to make mistakes and learn from them."

He looked a little dazed. Evidently he'd never encountered this reaction to his line before. It was a good line; it had even reached a part of her. But she'd been this route before. Jeff had showed her what being put on a pedestal could do to her. And she never wanted to be shown again. "Protected and cherished," she went on. "Those are nice-sounding words. But in reality, they make a prison, not a paradise."

That chin of his jutted out again and he shook his dark head. "There's no need to get so hyper. I meant that to be a compliment."

"I know," she said. "But that doesn't change

A Question of Trust 39

things. Compliments can be double-purposed. A protective cage keeps things *in* as well as *out*.''

She could almost see the gears shifting in his head. His frown cleared away and he grinned engagingly. ''I never thought of it that way. You're right, of course.''

I think he does understand. Why does this man appeal to me so?

She looked down. Her plate was empty. She had finished eating without even realizing it.

''How about some dessert?'' he asked, seeing the direction of her glance.

''No, thank you.'' *Be calm,* she told herself. *Be businesslike.* ''The dinner was excellent. But I have to get up early. There's some setting up to do before the cement truck comes. And, since we've finished our business discussion, I'd really like to go.''

''Of course.'' He finished his coffee and signaled to the waiter.

There was silence between them on the way back to her place, but it wasn't uncomfortable, at least not too uncomfortable. She fished her key out of her purse long before they reached the house and clutched it in clammy fingers. Vivid in her mind as they drove through the gathering dusk was the image of him bending toward her before they left the house. He had wanted to kiss her then and she had avoided him. But the evening had been

40   *Nina Coombs Pykare*

still before them. Now the evening was almost over. And . . .

I want him to kiss me. And that isn't like me. I don't know what to do.

He pulled into the drive and stopped beside the steps to the long veranda. "I really like this house," he said softly. "It's your kind of house. I mean it. It fits you perfectly."

Before she could say anything he came around and opened the door for her. His fingers were warm on her bare elbow as they moved together up the steps. At the door she turned and put out her hand. "Thank you for a lovely dinner," she said, her tone formal.

The expression on his face was amusing. If it hadn't been for her own inner turmoil, she might have been tempted to laugh. But when he accepted her hand without comment and shook it, she felt mingled disappointment and relief. *I guess, I . . .*

And then he used her hand to pull her into his arms. "Harrison, I—" But there was no time for more words. His mouth covered hers. Halfheartedly, she tried to protest, tried to wriggle free of his arms. But his grip on her was firm. One of his hands slid up under her hair to the nape of her neck, sending little shivers down her spine.

It wasn't a particularly long kiss and he didn't repeat it. When he released her mouth, he grinned,

A Question of Trust   41

that mischief in his eyes again. "That's better. This is the place for a woman—in a man's arms."

The nerve of the man! She jerked herself away. "You! You!" she sputtered, half angry, half amused. "Get out of here. Leave me alone."

His smile hardly changed; only his eyes narrowed a little. "Sorry, I can't grant your wish, sweetheart. See you on the job tomorrow. It's a very important job, you see. And I have to keep a close eye on it. A very close eye."

"Get out. Get . . ." She barely kept from bursting into laughter. He kissed his fingers and touched them to her parted lips. Only half playfully, she snapped her teeth shut.

"Till next time, sweetheart."

Then he was gone, leaping down the steps and climbing cheerfully into his car. It wasn't till he reached the road that she realized she was still standing there, the house key in her hand. *What have I gotten into now?* Harrison Green was a lot of fun. But love wasn't about fun. Love had to do with trust. And until she knew the man better, until she knew more about his connection to the City Council, love would have to wait.

Chapter Five

The next morning dawned clear and bright. Hustling out the door with her lunch pail in one hand, her big stainless thermos in the other, Terry stopped on the step to admire the lovely colors of the sky. *Thank you for another great sunrise. This one's really beautiful.*

Good thing she liked getting up early. Concrete construction wasn't work for those who wanted to sleep late.

She pulled in a deep breath of fresh morning air. This was her favorite time of day—when the neighborhood was just waking. A dog barked somewhere nearby and birds were singing their little hearts out in the big pine in the backyard. Yes, it was a wonderful world. *Thank you,* she said

A Question of Trust   43

again, and, laughing softly, swung down the back step.

The weather looked good, and they were well up to schedule. She set her lunch in the backseat and climbed in the old van. The municipal job was going well and she had plenty of other work lined up. It should be a really good summer for Matthews Concrete. Just as she'd hoped and planned.

She sighed, her smile fading. *Work* looked really good. But Harrison Green had thrown a monkey wrench into her personal life. She backed the big van out the drive and swung around toward the road. If only he wasn't quite so charming. If only his presence didn't unnerve her so much. If only she could be sure about his motives. *Stop it!* she told herself. *All these "if onlys" will get you nowhere. He may be terribly attractive, fun to be with, and all those other good things, but the man could be big trouble. If he's in with those crooks . . .*

A sudden lump formed in her throat. She'd be terribly disappointed if Harrison turned out to be implicated in this graft Pete had heard about. *Please, don't let him be crooked.* She straightened her shoulders and gritted her teeth. No matter how attractive he was, Harrison Green wouldn't get her to be dishonest.

She nosed the van into a parking spot at the site and climbed out. Tucking her knee boards under

44   *Nina Coombs Pykare*

one arm, and grabbing the tool bucket, she moved
off toward the pour. Probably Harrison was still
sound asleep. Those big executive types didn't get
up at the crack of dawn. Too bad. They missed so
much beauty. And a chance to feel really close to
nature.

A squirrel scurried partway down an oak and
peered at her from curious black eyes, its bushy
tail waving overhead. "Hello, there. Good morning to you, too." The squirrel ran up the oak and
out of sight. Fisher had saved most of the trees on
this site. That was the only thing she disliked about
construction, cutting down the old trees that had
so much dignity and beauty. But Fisher had managed to work around most of them here.

So Stonybrook's new municipal building would
be nestled in the middle of a beautiful park. She
liked that. The town was old, and small, but with
a charm all its own. Thank goodness, Fisher had
seen that charm, and not plunked some modern
monstrosity down in their midst. She liked Fisher.
He was a good man. For once the Council had
made a decent choice. *I guess I think the rumors*
are *true. I think they* are *crooks. But I don't want
them to be, especially not Harrison.*

She was still the only one at the site and she
breathed deeply, pulling in the rich earthy smells.
Some women, she supposed, would find the work
dirty and difficult, as Harrison had suggested.

A Question of Trust   45

Some would probably wrinkle their noses at the strange smells. But she loved every dirty, gritty bit of it, from the first estimate to that last finishing pass of the trowel and the proud moment she pressed down the mold that left the imprint MATTHEWS CONCRETE. Not a bad way to leave your mark on the world. In concrete. Good, strong buildings that would last.

She liked the business part, too—a good thing, because it was taking up more and more of her time. But not today—today she was going to work alongside the men. This was a big pour, and she'd arranged things so she could be there. Pete could have gotten an extra man from the next town over, of course, but he knew she liked to have a hand in things now and then. Just like he did.

A breeze tugged at her hair. Good thing she had Pete. He was old enough to be her father. In fact, he had several daughters her age. But he and she had always gotten along really well. Pete, at least, had no qualms about her being able to do her work. And he always treated her like the boss.

The sound of a familiar motor told her he was arriving. As he drove up in the truck with MATTHEWS CONCRETE in huge letters on the side she remembered the triumphant day she'd bought it, the pride she'd felt about the business, *her* business.

46 *Nina Coombs Pykare*

" 'Morning, Terry.'' Pete's craggy face lit with a cheery smile.

" 'Morning, Pete. Looks like a good day.''

"Yeah.'' He scratched his head. "Hope those extra eighteen-wheelers show like they promised. We got a big pour today.''

She nodded. The laborers who moved the power buggies, those big motor-run jobs that held three times as much concrete as a wheelbarrow, were really important on a job this size. With so much concrete involved, it had to be moved fast.

She chuckled. "How'd those buggies get to be called eighteen-wheelers? Do you know?''

Pete shrugged. "Nope. Somebody just started it and it hung on.''

He grinned at her, but his eyes were worried. "Say, Terry, you *sure* you're okay?''

She forced herself not to look away, not to be evasive with him. She was always honest. But she knew perfectly well what he was talking about. He was worried about the unprofessional way she'd treated Harrison Green. But she didn't want Pete to see how Green had gotten under her skin. And she didn't want him to mention the rumors about graft. She wished she'd never heard about the graft in the first place. Things would have been so different. "Why shouldn't I be all right?'' she asked.

"Well, yesterday.'' Pete practically shuffled his

A Question of Trust   47

feet in his embarrassment. "Well, you acted sort of strange."

She managed a weak smile. "I'm afraid Mr. Green and I didn't get along too well."

Pete didn't notice the past tense. "He seemed to like you *real* well."

Even though he made her feel a little embarrassed, she had to laugh at the eager look on his face. He was as bad as Mom, always matchmaking. "Pete, you know how men are. They have big egos."

Pete shook his head. "Naw, I don't think it's that. You know, Terry, a girl like you needs a husband." He hurried on, ignoring her frown. "I know, I know. You ain't got to tell me. You can take care of yourself. But you need someone to love. Can't all men be like that there dummy Jeff. Ought to be a man somewhere that'd fit the bill for you. Make you happy."

She smiled. Pete meant well. And he knew she was over Jeff. Otherwise he wouldn't have mentioned the man's name. "Well, I don't think that man is Harrison Green."

Pete looked away, so nonchalant she knew he was after something. "Nice-looking fellow, that Green though, ain't he?"

She laughed, hoping he couldn't tell that this very minute her heart was pounding at the thought of Harrison Green's good looks. "Yes, you old fox. Very nice-looking. But it's a man's character that counts. Looks aren't everything, you know.''

Pete grinned mischievously. ''Maybe not, but they're a lot.''

She just laughed. Pete's wife, Lucy, was a little thing, round-cheeked and very round-bodied, and it was obvious he loved her dearly. And no wonder. She was one of the best women around.

''Think he'll be coming by today?'' Pete asked, looking away again.

''Who?'' She pretended not to understand.

But Pete wasn't buying. He looked right at her and grinned. ''Green. Who else?''

She made a face. ''I sure hope not. The man's a pest.'' But even as she said it, she knew it wasn't entirely true. There was a part of her that wanted to see Harrison Green again. It wasn't a big part . . . well, not a very big part. But it was there. And she knew it.

She glanced up at the sky. Over the area where they stood, it was a clear brilliant blue, but to the west the horizon seemed a little dark. ''I hope it doesn't rain. Not today.''

Pete followed her gaze. ''Weatherman said clear and sunny. All the way through to the weekend.'' He scratched his head again and gave her a quizzical look. ''Think we can trust him?''

She laughed. ''I don't know. How many times have we heard that and gotten rained out?''

A Question of Trust   49

Pete laughed, too. "Too many. For sure. Them weathermen . . ." He shook his head. "Sometimes I think they throw darts or something. Don't seem like they really know anything 'bout what's really happening."

Chapter Six

The morning passed quickly. The hot sun soon had everyone stripped down to T-shirts. Around noon the men began to peel those off. Terry heaved a sigh. There were some disadvantages to being female that couldn't be overcome. She wiped her face on a big red work hankie and shoved it in the back pocket of her jeans.

So far Harrison Green hadn't shown. A good thing, too. She didn't have time to play his silly games. She stood up and rotated her neck from side to side. With a last appraising glance at the section of floor she was working, she went to get her lunch. Half an hour should be about right. When she got back, the concrete would be ready.

She took her lunch pail and thermos and went

A Question of Trust 51

to a big maple whose leaves gave protection from the sun. As she leaned back, her hard hat hit the tree with a clunk. She reached up and pulled it off. Sometimes she forgot she had it on. She ran her hand under the mass of her hair, clipped by a holder at the nape of her neck. Today was a hot one, all right. Her neck was soaked and her hair all damp.

She dropped the hard hat on the grass and reached in her lunch pail for a sandwich. Some sixth sense, some prickling of her nerves, warned her, so that seconds before he stopped in front of her she knew Harrison Green was coming.

"So," he said cheerfully from above her head. "Looks like my timing's just right."

She looked up. She couldn't very well keep staring at the man's well-worn engineer's boots. She wanted to say something witty, something that would let him know that last night's kiss had meant nothing, *less* than nothing, to her. The words were on the tip of her tongue, but nothing came out of her mouth. Those eyes of his were telling her plainly that he hadn't forgotten a single detail about last night and that it meant a lot to *him.*

"Mind if I join you?" He didn't wait for an answer, but dropped to the grass beside her. He was wearing blue jeans and a pale green sports shirt open at the throat. A wisp of brown hair curled there. Why did the man have to look so good? She didn't know any more about him than she had last night, but she definitely wanted to. And that wasn't smart.

She bit into her sandwich with a snap that made him raise a dark eyebrow. "I don't know who you're thinking of chewing up like that. But I'd say he'd better be careful." His lazy golden eyes laughed into hers.

He knew very well that he was getting to her. She could see it on his face. She chewed methodically, trying to ignore him and knowing it was impossible. No one could ignore Harrison Green.

He opened his carryout sack. "Want a piece of chicken?"

She shook her head. "No thanks. My lunch is fine."

He looked at her half-eaten sandwich and his grin widened. "Is that actually peanut butter and jelly?"

"It actually is." Why did he have to be so breathtakingly attractive? "It happens to keep well in hot weather. And in case you haven't noticed, there's no refrigeration on this job."

He smiled, that smile that almost made her forget her promises to herself. "You're a remarkable woman, Terry Matthews," he said. "A very remarkable woman."

A Question of Trust 53

She shrugged. "Because I know enough not to get food poisoning? Anyone should know that."

He shook that handsome head of his. "No, because you're such a bundle of contradictions. So beautiful and doing work like this. So feminine and inviting, yet . . ."

She laughed. "The only remarkable thing about me is that I finish what I start. I know what I want, and I go after it."

He nodded. "Well, we're alike in that." He grinned. "See, we're compatible already."

She munched away at her sandwich, determined to ignore his effect on her. Or at least to try.

"What about *who* you want? What's *he* like?" His voice had dropped to a lower tone, and the hair on the back of her neck stood up as though he'd touched her.

"There isn't anyone I want," she replied finally. "But if there were, first of all, he'd be honest."

He nodded, didn't seem surprised. What exactly did that mean?

"He'd be a good man, a man I could trust."

"And if you wanted him, you'd go after him." He made it a flat statement, not a question, but his eyes were challenging. "And if you did, he wouldn't have a chance, the poor sucker."

She tried to sound disgusted. "I don't see why my taste in men should be any business of yours."

Too late she saw the gleam in his eyes. "Oh, but it is, Terry. It's very much my business."

She wanted to say something bright and witty, but nothing would come. Her mind had gone completely blank. Her heart pounded and her mouth went dry, but words were lost to her. Methodically she finished the sandwich, tasteless now, and swallowed a mouthful of coffee. It was probably better, anyway, just to ignore him. She had an idea he was so good at this kind of word game that whatever she said, he would know how to twist it to what he wanted.

Hastily she swallowed the rest of the coffee and replaced the cap on the thermos. Closing up her lunch pail, she got to her feet.

"Awful short lunch hour." He raised another eyebrow.

Why was he here? What did he hope to gain from it?

She shrugged. "Concrete waits for no woman."

He chuckled. "My, you're sharp today."

She didn't feel sharp. She made her way back to the wagon to deposit her pail and thermos, feeling all thumbs, and very conscious of the way his look followed her. The scrutiny of those eyes made her nervous, made her want to order him off the site. Or, in a less civilized reaction, to kick him in the shins. What a shock that would be to the sophisticated Mr. Green!

A Question of Trust   55

Maybe she'd be lucky and he'd just go away. But as she turned back to the pour she could feel him still watching her. *Forget about the man,* she told herself, clapping her hard hat on her head. *You're here to finish concrete. Think about that. And nothing else.* She reached the piece she'd been working on and knelt to touch it. It yielded, but only a little. Good! It was about ready.

She got up and turned to get her knee boards. Good grief! Where had *he* come from? Harrison was standing there, looking completely at ease. And in hard hat and jeans he looked like he belonged here, right on the construction site. She could almost picture him with a trowel in his hand and—

''Don't they give you any work to do?'' she asked ungraciously. *What's wrong with me? Why does he rile me so?*

''This *is* my work.'' He refused to take offense, just kept smiling at her in that infuriating way.

''Besides,'' he went on, ''I like watching you finish concrete. It's a new experience for me.'' His eyes said even more than his words and she tried to ignore him, tried not to think of that kiss last night. Of course, that didn't work at all. She could hardly think of anything else. This was a new experience for her, too. No man had ever made her think about him so much, not even Jeff.

She'd better stop this foolishness and get to

work. Though she didn't relish having Harrison Green as an audience, it looked like she didn't have much choice. The concrete was setting up and if she didn't get to it soon, she was going to have a real mess on her hands. And she took pride in her work. It was the work she was meant to do, and she wanted to do it well.

Swallowing a sigh, she settled her padded knee boards on the concrete and got down. Being on her knees wasn't exactly the most comfortable position around Harrison Green. The man already made her feel weak and helpless. Down here, she also felt small and vulnerable. Too much like an old-fashioned woman. But she was doing honest work, she reminded herself, and that was enough.

Still, it was bad enough to face Harrison standing up, when he was only three or four inches taller. Well, she wouldn't look up. She'd just do her work and ignore the man.

Chapter Seven

Trouble was, ignoring Harrison Green wasn't such an easy thing to do. Though Terry didn't look at him, though she tried hard to concentrate on the concrete in front of her, she couldn't forget he was there, his golden eyes watching her every move.

She took it as long as she could, the tension building in her till she wanted to scream, till even her silent prayers for help couldn't calm her. Then in exasperation, she threw down her trowel and stood up. "Green!"

"Yes, Matthews?" He moved around so she could see him.

The sparkle in his eyes warned her, but she couldn't stop herself. "Will you kindly get out of here?"

His face broke into a grin. ''Temper, temper, Matthews. What would that wonderful man think? You know, the one you're planning to marry someday.''

She could tell he was enjoying himself immensely, but this was no joking matter. Her temper flared. It was one of the things about herself she'd tried to reform. Not too successfully. At least, not around him. She counted silently to ten. *Please, I need help with this,* she prayed.

''Goodness,'' Harrison went on smugly. ''You might corrupt my morals.''

Her snort was as unladylike as her feelings. ''Morals? You have the morals of an alley cat!'' Now why had she said that? He hadn't done anything to deserve it and it might let him know she suspected him, that she was on to the graft thing.

His eyes darkened, but he only smiled. ''Sorry, I didn't realize my being here would interfere with your work. Do I bother you that much?'' He asked the question innocently enough, but his smile came dangerously close to a smirk.

She snorted again. ''You have the most colossal ego I've ever seen.'' She shrugged. ''Watch all you like. I just think it's a pity the city pays you good money to stand around wasting your time. Someone ought to alert the taxpayers to what you're doing.''

He just went on grinning, the irritating . . . And

A Question of Trust 59

then he said, ''Wouldn't do any good to bother the taxpayers. Remember, I'm not elected. Besides, I assure you, from my point of view, this is a very profitable activity.''

She threw up her hands in disgust. ''Great! Be my guest. Watch all you like. Just keep out of my way!'' Turning her back on him, she plopped down on the knee boards with a force that made her knees ache. Too bad she didn't have some heavy straightedging to do. She grabbed her trowel. Anger like this could provide some good energy. No sense wasting it.

I know this man is here for a purpose. I just don't know what it is. And he's so aggravating.

He stood there to one side of her for long minutes while she forced herself to work the concrete—carefully, patiently. She looked up once and his boots were gone, out of her line of vision. But before she could draw a deep breath of relief, she realized that he hadn't left. He'd only moved around behind her.

Grinding her teeth, she went on working the concrete, carefully passing the trowel over its surface. She'd have to stick it out. Maybe he'd tire of the game, finally, and leave her alone. *That would help. I don't know how to relate to him. I like him. I like him too much. Please, don't let him be part of the graft. Please.*

The minutes passed. They seemed like hours,

60   *Nina Coombs Pykare*

like this game of his would go on forever and forever. But she worked and she prayed. And then,
when she was almost done, a long low whistle echoed behind her. Several very unflattering phrases
came to her mind, things she'd never dream of
saying out loud, things she seldom even thought.
*He really pushed my buttons. And I don't know
why.* She shut her mouth firmly and went on working concrete. He wasn't going to get a rise out her
again. He wasn't. He wasn't.

The prickling hairs on the back of her neck told
her that he was still standing there. Her face was
flushed, far more than could be accounted for even
by the heat. She could feel beads of perspiration
standing on her upper lip, but she didn't dare to
stop and wipe her face. If she met his eyes now . . .

*It makes me mad to admit it, but he's raising
other feelings besides anger in me. He's making
me think crazy, weird thoughts about spending my
life with him, about that line of golden-eyed
children.*

Stop it, she told herself. *Remember the rumors.
You don't know anything about the man, except
that he's probably trouble.*

Trouble's boots came back into view and waited
patiently. "What's the matter, Terry?" he asked.

She forced herself to look up. He was smiling,
that cat-in-the-cream smile that she found so in-

A Question of Trust   61

furiating. Only half aware of what she was doing, she struggled to her feet. ''Nothing's the matter.''

She took a deep breath to steady herself. He was awfully close, as close as he'd been the night before. Close enough to kiss her. She pushed the thought away, but it didn't want to go.

For a long silent moment she stared into his golden eyes, willing herself not to be pulled in, not to surrender. But they were magic. And nothing seemed to defend her against their power.

''Terry.'' Her name was a mere whisper on his lips, a soft, inviting whisper. She had to do something. Her heart pounded, seemed stuck in her throat. Her lungs didn't want to pull in air. If she didn't move, if she didn't get away from him . . . He was going to kiss her, right here in the middle of the construction site. In front of the crew. And if he did, she'd never be able to face the men. After a thing like that, they wouldn't see her as boss.

''Look, you'd better—'' But she never got to finish the sentence.

He reached out and, when his hand grazed her arm, she actually jumped. It *was* like an electric shock. *Crazy, I've gone crazy.*

''Terry, I . . .'' Harrison took a step toward her and the panic inside her swelled. If she didn't get away, she'd be lost forever, pulled into those golden eyes and drowned. And all her promises to herself would be broken.

She stepped backward. Her boot heel brushed the edge of the form, she was going to fall! There was no way to stop herself, but she reached out automatically, grabbing for something, anything, the nearest object—Harrison Green.

She went over backward to the sound of ripping material. She hit the freshly troweled concrete with a plop. At least it hadn't completely set. But then she stopped thinking about concrete because Harrison Green landed, too. Right smack on top of her.

She tried to breathe. All the air was gone from her lungs, but she wasn't sure if it was because of the fall or because of Harrison. He raised his head. Concrete speckled his chin, his nose, his dark eyebrows, She wanted to laugh, but she had no breath to do it with.

It was just as well, for the look in his eyes was threatening. ''If I thought,'' he began, ''that you did this to me on purpose . . .''

''I'm here, too,'' she pointed out, hating the sound of her breathlessness. ''And on the bottom.''

His eyes changed, lightened. ''Yes, indeed. So you are.''

''Harrison, I don't think—''

''That's right,'' he said softly. ''Don't think. Just feel.''

She was feeling too much already. Way too much. ''But . . .''

A Question of Trust 63

Her words died as she saw his mouth coming toward hers. She tried to turn away from him, but her hard hat was stuck in the concrete, holding her head in the same position. If he kissed her now . . .

"It's no use," he muttered. "I can't fight it. Neither can you."

She couldn't find the breath to answer him. And in any case it wouldn't have mattered. His mouth covered hers and everything else faded from existence.

When he raised his head, she was dazed, groggy with feelings. "Oh," he said. "What you do to me."

Oh, no! She was lying in wet concrete and he'd been kissing her. Worse, she'd been kissing him back. "Get up, you big oaf. You're crushing me."

His eyes gleamed. "But it's delightful, isn't it?"

"Get up! Get off me!"

"Now, now, Terry. It's not that bad, is it?"

Really it wasn't, but she couldn't tell him that. She struggled for words. "This is concrete we're lying in, you know. It hardens. Really hardens." Her hair would be full of it. "Get up."

He smiled down at her, his mouth only inches away. "I'm perfectly comfortable right here. And the view is terrific. Why, I could stay here all day. Unless you want to admit it isn't so bad."

He was so stubborn. And so close. "I . . . all

right, all right. It isn't so bad. Now, can we get up?"

He kissed the tip of her nose, getting concrete on her chin, too. "First, I think you ought to tell me you're sorry."

Had the man lost his senses? "Sorry? What on earth for?"

"For pulling me into this mess with you. On the other hand . . ." His eyes grew speculative. "Maybe you're not sorry. Maybe you did it on purpose."

She pushed against his shoulders with her hands, hands covered with wet concrete. "I'm sorry. I'm sorry. Now, let me up. It'll take me hours just to get the concrete out of my hair."

"You were going to wash it anyway, remember?" His eyes burned into hers. "I'll be glad to come around to the house and help you. We could help each other."

His eyes glowed with that look that made her want to melt. Had she thought he was dangerous? This man was deadly! "Up!" she repeated. "I'll wash my own hair, thank you."

Heaving a great sigh, he kissed the tip of her nose again and pushed himself to his feet.

She drew in a deep breath. It was silly to feel that she'd lost something when he got up. She'd never *had* anything with this man. This was the man she knew nothing about, except that she sus-

A Question of Trust   65

pected him of taking graft. *I have to remember that. I have to.*

She sighed again, took the hand he extended to her, and let him pull her to her feet. She took off her hard hat and tried to shake out her hair. Harrison Green made her feel like no man ever had, like she wanted to share her life with him. And that was the most dangerous thing of all.

Standing there, with splotches of concrete all over him, he was still the most attractive man she'd ever seen. And the way he looked at her— *Help me,* she prayed. *Help me resist him.*

"You'd better go home and shower right away," she told him. "This stuff is hard to get out. And it'll irritate your skin."

"And you?" His eyes went to her hair. It must be a real mess, but his expression didn't say that, it said . . . She couldn't think about that now.

"I'll call someone to fix this piece of concrete. And then I'll go home and wash up." Unable to bear the look in his eyes, she turned away.

"Okay. See you tonight."

She swung around again. "Tonight?" Oh dear, why did she have to sound so happy about it?

He grinned, that smug grin of his. "Sure. Same time. We have more business to discuss."

"Business? But Harrison . . ."

He was already gone, hurrying away toward his car. Frustrated again, and muttering under her breath, she went to look for Pete.

Chapter Eight

Later that evening Terry stood in front of her closet. She grinned. Harrison had said they had business to discuss—maybe she'd just hold him to that. She took out her black suit, a tailored white blouse, and the pumps. *Yes, I'll hold him to business. If I can.*

Her stomach rolled over and then righted itself again. Unless he meant to use tonight to bring up the subject of graft. Maybe last night he'd been trying to soften her up, and tonight he'd move in for the kill, tell her about the kickback and how much she was supposed to hand over to him. But this was sure a funny way to do it.

She plopped down on the bed and pulled on her pantyhose, slipping her feet into her black pumps.

A Question of Trust   67

Don't let him talk graft tonight. Don't let him talk graft ever. Let him be an honest man. Please.

Slipping into her blouse and skirt, she went to the mirror to button them, shaking her head at her reflection. It was impossible not to notice the flush on her cheeks, the sparkle in her eyes. There was no denying it—Harrison Green had already made a difference in her life. A big difference.

But I can't be thinking how much I like the man. I can't let him sneak into even the tiniest corner of my heart. Because if I do, he'll soon have it all.

And what if he did? She had no proof he was in on the graft. He seemed so honest, so straight-forward. In some ways he reminded her of Dad. She liked Harrison. Oh boy, did she like him!

She laughed a little, not too bitterly. Hadn't she liked Jeff, trusted him, meant to share the rest of her life with him? And look how that had turned out!

No. She pulled her severe black business bag from the drawer. When it came to an attractive man's character, she just had to admit it, she wasn't such a good judge. It'd be better to take a wait-and-see attitude. Maybe time would prove that Harrison *was* what he said he was—a man doing his job. Doing it with a certain air of mischief, of course, but an essentially honest man.

I hope time proves that. But if it doesn't, I'll

still be all right. Because I intend to keep my heart intact. I have to.

The shrilling of the phone made her almost leap out of her shoes. Could that be Harrison? What if he canceled? She dropped her bag on the couch and ran to the phone. ''Hello?''

''Terry?''

''Mom. Hi.'' She heaved a great sigh of relief. ''How are you?''

''Okay, dear.''

There was something different in Mom's voice, something not quite right. ''Mom, what's wrong?''

Mom laughed, a nervous laugh not like her usual happy trill. ''Nothing, dear. Really. It's just— well—I've met this wonderful man.''

Terry laughed, too. ''Is that all? Come on, Mom. I know Dad's been gone a long time. I'm not going to get all bent out of shape because you go out to dinner with a man.''

Mom chuckled, but she still sounded nervous. ''Well, dear, that's good. It's just that Tom thought, well, he wanted—''

Mom was a dear, but once she got an idea in her head, she couldn't be moved. ''Mom, it's okay. Really. You're still coming up to visit, aren't you? Like you promised?''

''Yes, dear. I'm afraid Florida is just too hot for me in the summer. I thought maybe in a couple of weeks. If that's okay with you.''

A Question of Trust   69

"It's great, Mom. I'm looking forward to it."
Terry looked at her watch. "Listen, I'm just getting ready to go out. Can we—"

"Out? Out with a man?"

Terry frowned at herself in the mirror. Mom had never given up trying to marry her off. "Yes, Mom. Out with a man. But it's only business." Well, that *had* been what he said. "He's the new city manager. We're going to talk about the municipal building. You remember, I told you about it, that big job I got. It's just a business dinner."

"Oh." Mom's sigh said a lot more than the little word.

Terry bit her lip. *I'm sorry to disappoint Mom, but it is* my *life.*

"Oh, I thought maybe—"

"I know what you thought, Mom. But this isn't a date." *That's not a lie. I don't think it's a date. I can't let it be a date.* "You've just got to be patient, Mom. I'll get married eventually. All in good time."

Why should saying that make her heart beat faster now? She'd said it many times before. Many, many times.

"Well, I hope so! I want to be a grandmother, you know."

"You will, you will. Now I've got to go."

"Yes, dear. Have a good time. I'll call when I get my flight number. 'Bye."

" 'Bye."

Terry stood there, the phone still in her hand, seeing herself with a baby in her arms, a baby with golden eyes and an irresistible smile. And then she could see a whole row of dark-haired children, and every last one of them had Harrison Green's golden eyes!

Not again! She shook herself. This was ridiculous. So he wanted children, too. So what? *Forget these silly daydreams. There's no point in them.*

Thank goodness she hadn't told Mom much about Harrison. Mom's imagination had no bounds—at least where things romantic were concerned. One date and Mom would have her at the altar already.

Terry glanced at the clock. Five till seven. Maybe this suit wasn't such a good idea. Did she still have time to change . . . ?

The doorbell rang. There he was. She smoothed the French knot that held her hair, pinned a smile on her lips, and went to the door.

He couldn't hide the disappointment on his face. "Do you have to wear that thing? I expected something more festive."

Hiding a smile, she shrugged. "You did say *business*. I dressed accordingly."

"So I see. Well, I suppose it can't be helped."

He looked marvelous in his dinner jacket. But then he looked marvelous in anything. Maybe she

A Question of Trust

should have worn something else, something more . . . but it was too late for that. "What did you have in mind?"

"Just dinner. Maybe some place with a little music." He grinned. "Do you like to dance?"

She hesitated. She loved to dance, and she hadn't gone dancing for a long time. Not since Jeff had . . . But this wasn't the time for it. Or the man. Not till she was surer of him, of what kind of man he was. "This is a business meeting. Surely dancing isn't called for."

He shrugged again. He did have the broadest shoulders. "There you go again with your double standard."

"*My* double standard?" She couldn't hold back a chuckle. "What are you talking about? Surely you're not going to tell me that if I were a man, you'd want to dance with me!"

He looked startled, and then he chuckled, too. "Of course not."

"Then, if you expect to conduct business with me like a man, you mustn't ask me to do unmanly things." She had him now. What could he say to that?

But instead of following her lead, he reached over and captured her hand. His eyes gazed into hers. "Terry, you know very well that what I want from you has nothing to do with business. Nothing at all."

Her heart jumped up in her throat. "You mean you admit—"

"I admit to being fascinated by you," he said, his voice low and husky. "I admit to using every means at my disposal to get your attention. Is there something wrong with that?"

"I . . ." She didn't know how to answer. Maybe not—if he wasn't part of the graft thing. But she had no way to know, no way to find out. After all, she couldn't just come out and *ask* the man.

"I don't know," she said with a little laugh. "But I should tell you—my dating skills are rusty."

"That's good," he said. "So are mine."

Chapter Nine

The restaurant was small and intimate—tiny white-covered tables, each lit by a single candle— the kind of place a man took a woman he wanted to impress, or maybe propose to. *I shouldn't be thinking things like that. I should be thinking business. Business, nothing but business.*

Across the little table Harrison's eyes glowed at her. "I see you got the concrete out of your hair." He grinned.

She couldn't help smiling a little. "Yes, but it was no picnic. When that stuff sets up, it's like—"

"Concrete." His chuckle was warm and deep. "I know. It took me quite a while to get it all off."

"Right." She took a deep breath. *Business. Help me remember business. Please,* she prayed

74 *Nina Coombs Pykare*

silently. "What about this business you wanted to discuss with me?"

He made a face. "You mean you're going to make me walk the straight and narrow?"

She laughed. "Oh, yes. You said business."

He shook his head. "All right, all right. Business it is."

Now why did she feel disappointed? Well, for one thing, though she might not know him well, she did know it wasn't like him to give in so easily. "And?"

His grin grew wider. "How about I make you a deal?"

Her heart missed a beat. Was it coming now? Was he going to make this graft thing into some kind of joke? She swallowed and forced the words out. "What kind of deal?"

"We review all the specs and—"

Relief washed over her. "Specs again! I told you—"

"I know. It must be awfully aggravating." He covered her hand with his. She should pull away. But she didn't. She just sat there, letting herself feel his fingers on hers.

"But Toohey has this bee in his bonnet," Harrison went on. "He wants me to go over everything, see if you can save the city some money."

She let her breath out slowly. Toohey again. Was this some kind of lead-in to the graft? Did

A Question of Trust   75

they mean to make it impossible for her to do her work unless she cooperated with them?

Well, she was her own woman. And all she could tell anyone—even Harrison—was the truth. ''I made my bid. The city accepted my bid. I'm sticking to the terms of the contract. The inspectors know me; they'll all tell you that.''

She had a notion to add that the only money Toohey was ever interested in saving was money headed for *his* pocket, but she bit her lip and didn't say it. She didn't know that—not for sure. And she wouldn't say anything about a person that might not be true.

She swallowed a sigh. Maybe Harrison wasn't going to talk about graft. Maybe it was something else.

''I know all that. Believe me.'' He shifted uncomfortably in his chair. ''But Toohey's my boss—one of them, anyway. And I more or less have to do what he tells me to do.''

She made a face, and he chuckled. ''You're right. Toohey's a windbag. But anyway, let's just run over the list he gave me.'' He patted his pocket. ''Then I can tell Toohey I did my thing. And he'll be happy.''

''Fine.'' Her tone was frosty. *Just thinking about graft makes me sick. And if there isn't any graft, then Toohey's still a pompous windbag who has no business running anything. Sorry. I did it again. Judging.* She pulled in a deep breath. If Harrison was going to talk graft, they might as well get it over with. "So, what's the deal?"

His fingers tightened around hers. "I'll make it as quick as possible, and I'll give Toohey your answers word for word."

"Huh!" She snorted. "You can tell him—"

"Well, maybe not word for word." Harrison grinned. "I'll soften it a little, be diplomatic. You know."

Her breath caught in her throat. The deal! He hadn't gotten to the rest of the deal. "And then?"

"And then we'll spend the rest of the evening dancing."

"Dancing?" she repeated stupidly. What did dancing have to do with kickbacks?

"Yes." He leaned toward her, his eyes gleaming in the candlelight. "That's why I came to this place. They play soft romantic music—the big band sound. You do like the big bands?"

"I—" It was hard to shift gears so quickly. She'd been expecting him to talk graft, and he wanted to dance!

He was staring at her intently. "Well?"

"Yes," she said. "I like to dance."

He gave her one of those mischievous grins. "Thank goodness. For a minute there I thought we were incompatible."

If he only knew what she'd been thinking! For

A Question of Trust 77

a minute she actually considered telling him. Then common sense intervened and she clamped her lips shut. True, he hadn't mentioned graft—not yet. But that didn't mean he wasn't in on it. Her reputation for honesty was pretty well known. Maybe the crooks had sent him to keep an eye on her, to prevent her from seeing or hearing something she shouldn't.

He squeezed her fingers again and she felt a pang of remorse. She was suspecting him of terrible things—and he might be the most honest man in the world! But that was what dishonesty did to people. It corrupted everything it touched and turned people against one another. *I hope he's not bad. I hope, oh please, let him be the good man I want him to be.*

"Hey." Harrison touched her cheek. "No need to look so serious. If you don't want to dance, it's okay. No big deal."

But it *was* a big deal. She could tell from his face that he was disappointed.

She took a deep breath. Well, dancing wasn't dishonest. And Harrison hadn't even *done* anything suspicious. Maybe she was letting her imagination run away with her, and all because of those silly rumors.

Toohey had made a lot of her life uncomfortable already. Why should she let him spoil her first night of fun in a long time? That settled it. She wouldn't.

"Okay," she said. "It's a deal. Bring on the questions."

His smile was so bright she almost changed her mind. How could just the chance to dance with her make the man that happy? And why did *she* feel so good? Happy, wanting to laugh so much, to laugh and talk to him? About anything. About everything.

"Great." He pulled out the list.

Chapter Ten

By the time their meal was over—an excellent meal of swordfish, scalloped potatoes, and broccoli—they had gone over all of Toohey's questions.

"All done." Harrison tucked the list back in his pocket. "Do you want dessert now or later?"

"Later." She motioned toward the band in their alcove. "The music's getting to me."

"Me too. So shall we?"

She let him take her hand and lead her to the dance floor, but even before they got there she wasn't sure it was such a good idea. Maybe this deal of his was a mistake. Slow dancing meant close dancing. And being close to Harrison Green was bound to mean trouble.

Still, if she tried to back out, he'd want to know why. And she couldn't tell him. She didn't want to talk about graft and kickbacks. If she mentioned them, he might think she was hinting at some kind of deal. Or even worse, he might offer her one. And what she'd been afraid of would come to pass.

At the dance floor, he turned and she stepped into his arms. The music was mellow, and her heart slowed its pounding and grew calmer. His arms were warm around her, warm and strong. She felt right there. She wanted to move closer, to lay her head on his shoulder and . . .

The music swirled around them, pulling her back to another, more romantic time. The vocalist sang of memories and kisses. Terry let herself go with the music, let it surround her and sweep her along.

"Tell me about the first time you worked concrete." His lips were so near her ear that it took a while for his words to register. When they did, she looked up into his face. That was a mistake. His face was so close. And his lips . . . She turned away, looking back over his shoulder. "I—why do you want to hear about that?"

"I want to hear all about you, Terry. You fascinate me."

Well, her childhood was a safe topic. At least he wasn't asking about her love life or checking

A Question of Trust 81

out the gossip he'd probably heard about her and Jeff. And he wasn't talking about graft.

"Let me think. I guess I was about five. It was summer, and Dad took me to the job with him."

Harrison led her easily around the floor. Dancing with him didn't take any thought. It was like she'd done it a thousand times before. "Did your mother go out to work?" he asked.

She glanced at him in surprise. "Oh no, she was always home. But I wanted to go to work with Dad. Like my boy cousins went with *their* dad. I wanted it so bad that I begged and begged. And finally Dad took me."

Her cheek against his shoulder, she called up her memories. "It was a small job that first time. A little patio that took only half a day. He gave me my own knee pads and trowel—and a corner of concrete to work. And he showed me what to do."

She sighed into his shoulder. "Oh, it was marvelous. After that, I worked with Dad every chance I got. When I got older, I worked summers with him. I learned all about the business, right there beside him. He was a fine man—a good, kind man."

She swallowed hard, blinking back the tears. "And then he had a heart attack and just like that, he was—gone."

Her voice broke on the last word and Harrison's

arms tightened around her in comfort. "I'm sorry," he said. "You must miss him a lot."

"Yes." She didn't pull away, didn't deny her feelings. It was good to be in Harrison's arms, good to have someone who understood. She swallowed again. "Dad was my hero, I guess. He was honest and good. He didn't talk a lot, didn't say much, but he built things, things that lasted. And he helped people. Every chance he got, he helped people."

"You're lucky."

The pain in his voice startled her into looking up into his face again. His eyes were dark with sympathy—and something else.

"You're lucky you had a father who loved you," he said. "And lucky his passing was quick."

"What about your parents?"

"Both gone. Mom in an accident. That was quick, thank goodness. But Dad—"

She could see he didn't want to talk about it. "It's all right. I understand."

"You said you're an only child," he went on, accepting the change of subject.

"Yes." She tried a little chuckle. "I didn't like it much. I wanted someone to play with."

A little of the light came back into his eyes. "I suppose that could be lonely. I never got to find

A Question of Trust 83

out. Had two brothers and a sister. All younger.''
He grinned. "All little pests.''

She laughed with him. "Yet you said you want
children.''

He smiled. "Of course I do.''

"How many?''

"Oh, six or eight.''

She stared up at him. "You've got to be kid-
ding. How could you raise that many these days?''

He looked thoughtful. "Well, at least two or
three.''

"Not three.''

"Why not? I can support three kids.''

"Oh, that isn't it. It's just—well.'' She wished
she hadn't mentioned it, but she knew he wouldn't
let it pass. "It's just that I had two girl cousins,
both a little older. That made three of us. And we
were always splitting up. Two against one.'' She
shivered, and he pulled her closer. "It's not a good
feeling to be cut out.''

"I suppose not. I was too busy refereeing fights
to find out.''

His arm tightened around her protectively. She
didn't want him to think . . . "Of course, it wasn't
always me that was odd man out.''

There was comfort in his voice when he said,
"Of course not.'' But that didn't mean he believed
her. Now he'd be doing more psychoanalyzing,
thinking she'd wanted to do boy things because

84   *Nina Coombs Pykare*

the girls shut her out of their play. But it wasn't that, not really. She'd liked playing with dolls, but she didn't want to wait around for the daddy to come home from work. She wanted to do something herself, something that would last.

"Do you like working for the city?"

The question was so much off what they'd been talking about that for a moment she couldn't think, even missed a step and tramped on his toes. "Sorry, you took me by surprise. Working for the city is all right, I guess. Toohey, though—"

Harrison nodded. "I know. I've spent enough time with him to understand his character."

In spite of herself she asked, "His character?"

"Sure. That's what I do. I study people. Their characters. What makes them tick."

"Like you do me."

He grinned. "Well, you're a special case. But sort of like that."

"Oh."

"Yes, I guess if I hadn't gone into city government, I'd have trained in psychology. Anyway, I know Toohey's type."

She waited, but he didn't go on, just held her close while they danced, and hummed softly in her ear. Finally she prompted him. "What *is* Toohey's type?"

"Do you really want to talk about Toohey now?" Harrison asked. "I'd rather talk about us."

A Question of Trust   85

So would I. But I can't let my feelings carry me away, not when I don't know . . . "I *am* talking about us—or at least you," she said. "Come on, Doctor, give me your analysis of Toohey. I want to see how good you are at this."

He didn't look too happy about it, but he said, "Oh, all right, if you insist. I see Toohey as a throwback to the old days. He'd have made a great Boss Tweed."

She swallowed, wishing she hadn't brought this on herself, wishing she'd let him talk about her. But she hadn't. And he'd said that about Toohey. They might as well get it out in the open. "You mean he's corrupt."

Harrison coughed and looked a little sheepish. "Don't put words in my mouth now." He frowned. "And don't let anyone else hear you say that. Toohey, well, Toohey's Toohey. He likes power. He likes money. And in his position—"

"It's relatively easy to get both."

"More or less."

"Well, Doctor, I'm afraid I agree with you. And that makes working with the city not such a pleasant experience. Still, Fisher's good—a fine architect. I like what he's doing with the building."

Harrison nodded. "I've studied the plans. He's a good man. Careful of the surrounding landscape. I like that. I hate seeing old trees cut down. It seems such a waste."

"I know."

Nina Coombs Pykare

* * *

They danced until she said she had to go home, longer, really, than they should have. Then they rode back to her place in silence. But not really, because she could still hear the music. The sweet strains of violins, the throbs of trombones and saxes. The melodies played on and on in her head—melodies of love, melodies of forever.

I need to stop this, to get out of this dreaminess. I'm a businesswoman coming back from a business dinner. A little romantic music, a few dances, isn't going to change that. And besides, I don't know about . . .

The house looked soft and inviting in the moonlight, a place for a family. A cool breeze blew from the west and the night sky sparkled with stars.

"Beautiful, isn't it?" he said, reaching for her hand. "God outdid himself when he made the sky."

"Yes. I've always loved a clear night. There's something about the stars, something that brings us closer to the universe." That dreamy sound in her voice was a dead giveaway. The music had really gotten to her.

She had to pull herself together. They reached the door. "Thank you for the dinner. And the dancing. I enjoyed it."

"Not as much as I did."

"But—"

A Question of Trust 87

"I know. Tomorrow's a working day."

"Yes, I—"

"Then"—he pulled her close—"I'll just kiss you and be on my way."

His arms were warm and his lips gentle. She kissed him back. There was no harm in it. Just a little thank-you kiss. Just for this night, this one night, she wanted to put aside all these stupid suspicions.

He raised his head and the moonlight made his eyes into golden pools of emotion. "Good night, Terry." His voice was deep, husky. "See you soon."

"Soon," she echoed. And then he was gone, striding back to his car. And the melody of the song they'd danced to earlier played on in her head.

Chapter Eleven

Around ten the next morning the phone rang. Terry picked it out of the welter of bills and estimates littering her desk. "Matthews Concrete. Terry speaking."

"Miss Matthews, this is Councilman Toohey's secretary."

Terry swallowed a groan. *Why can't Toohey leave me alone? What does the man want now?* She took a deep breath. "Yes, Miss Ferris?"

"Councilman Toohey expects you at a meeting for one o'clock this afternoon."

Not again! "A meeting about what?"

Miss Ferris's voice took on an evasive quality. "I'm sorry, I don't know what it's about. But he asked that you be prompt."

A Question of Trust 89

"Prompt?" Terry kept herself from yelling, but just barely. *I know it isn't her fault.* But that wasn't so easy to remember. "I'd at least like some idea of what the meeting's about. How can I know what to bring?"

Miss Ferris let out a huge sigh. "I'm sorry, Miss Matthews. That's all I know."

"All right." Terry put the phone down extra carefully. What good would it do to slam it? Had Harrison told Toohey what she'd said about him? If he had . . . Toohey was hard enough to deal with as it was. But surely Harrison hadn't done anything like that. Why, last night—

She jumped to her feet. She couldn't sit around mooning over dancing with Harrison. She had to get together every bit of paper she had on the municipal job. There was no telling what kind of questions Toohey would ask her. And she meant to be prepared.

At five till one, wearing a standard business suit and another severe blouse, Terry entered Toohey's outer office. It was empty. She frowned and sat down, dropping her briefcase on the floor beside her. It bulged with everything and anything Toohey might ask for. And she was madder than . . . She couldn't think of a word strong enough. Her whole morning had been spent collecting this stuff, a morning wasted. And the afternoon would be wasted, too. She could have been doing other things with her time, lots of other things. Toohey was the most pompous, irritating—

She bowed her head. *I need to be calm. There's probably something I'm supposed to learn from this. Patience, maybe? I know I'm short on that.*

Feeling better, she raised her head. But the better feelings didn't last. Where were the councilmen? Weren't they supposed to be there, too? She didn't want to face Toohey alone. Not that she was scared of him. But it wouldn't get her any points with the Council to go decking a councilman. And she would love to deck Toohey, if he got out of line. She looked down at the briefcase. Loaded as it was, it would make a hefty weapon. She picked it up.

"Looks like a lethal weapon."

"Harrison! Hello." She smiled as he came into the room. In a pale brown summer-weight suit, with a peach-colored shirt and a solid chocolate-colored tie, he looked so good she wanted to kiss him. *Business,* she reminded herself. *Think about business.* "Did Toohey call you to the meeting, too?"

Harrison frowned. "Toohey called you in?"

She nodded. "Yes, but I've no idea why. Miss Ferris didn't know." She hefted the briefcase again. "That's why I'm lugging all this."

The puzzlement on his face made her stomach

A Question of Trust 91

roil uneasily. "Did he tell *you* what he wanted?" she asked.

"No-o. He didn't call me for a meeting. I just stopped around to report to our esteemed councilman—on my conversation last night with you."

"But—You mean you haven't seen him since before last night?"

Harrison nodded, his expression growing more serious. "That's right. Listen—"

The door opened and Miss Ferris appeared, her thin nose twitching nervously. She looked toward Terry, as usual not at her face but over her shoulder. "Miss Matthews, Mr. Toohey will see you now."

Terry got to her feet. Time to face the dragon in his den. *Please help me be strong. And to hold my temper.* "Fine," she said.

Harrison took her by the elbow and before she knew what was happening, propelled her into Toohey's inner office. Behind them Miss Ferris stammered, "But, but, Mr.—"

When Harrison opened the door, a blast of cold air hit Terry. She shivered, grateful for her jacket. But then, she'd known what to expect. Toohey kept his office too cold for most people. A hulk of a man with three chins and a belly that went far beyond beer, he slouched in an expensive silk suit behind a gigantic eight-foot desk topped with gleaming glass. His right hand, a huge diamond glittering on his little finger, held a fat cigar, and gray smoke encircled his head, giving him the look of a brooding, corpulent demon.

"Come in, Matt—" He stopped and glared in surprise. "Green! What're you doing here?"

Harrison seemed not to notice anything unusual in Toohey's not-so-pleasant greeting. Harrison settled comfortably in a chair near the huge desk. "Stopped by to bring you the list, sir—you know, the answers to the questions you had about the municipal job." He leaned back and crossed his legs, the picture of relaxation.

Terry looked around. Sit or stand? Sitting seemed better. More relaxed. Even though there was no chair set for her, she took one, tried to lean back and look relaxed like Harrison.

Scowling, Toohey stabbed the smelly cigar at Harrison. "Yes, yes, you could've left your list with Ferris."

Harrison leaned forward again, all eagerness. "Yes, sir, I could have, sir, but I knew how anxious you were for these results. So I thought I'd just come along in with Miss Matthews. And together we could answer all your questions, satisfy your mind."

Toohey shifted his bulk, his beady little eyes moving nervously from one to the other. "Not necessary. I can talk to her myself."

A Question of Trust 93

"Oh, I know that, sir. I certainly know that. I just want to do my job. You know how it is."

Terry swallowed an urge to giggle. Harrison was taking this eager-to-please thing a little too far, making it into a caricature almost. But Toohey didn't seem to be aware of what was going on.

"And since you put me in charge of this job," Harrison went on, "I want to do all I can."

Toohey's face went from pink to red. It was obvious he wasn't going to discuss whatever he'd called her in for in front of Harrison. Now what? She sure didn't want to be alone with Toohey. But she didn't want to have to do this all over again and lose another day's work. What a pain. This city job was becoming a bad deal. Maybe she shouldn't have taken it.

But it was too late now. She might as well get it over with. Turning to Harrison, she smiled as sweetly as she could. "I'm sure I can answer any questions Councilman Toohey has, Mr. Green. So why don't you run along? You must have a lot of work to do."

For a second, puzzlement shone in Harrison's eyes. He stared at her so long she thought he was going to make a scene and refuse to leave. But then he grinned and unfolded himself from the chair. "Of course, Miss Matthews. See you later."

Sort of surprised that he'd given in so easily, she waited till the door closed behind him, then

94 *Nina Coombs Pykare*

took a deep breath. Facing Toohey, she asked, ''Now, Councilman, what is it you want to know?''

An hour later, Terry emerged from Toohey's office. In spite of the coldness in there, she felt wilted and wrung out. *I made it without losing my temper. I wasn't sure I could do it, but I did.*

She kept her expression carefully neutral as she passed the secretary's desk. ''Good-bye, Miss Ferris. Have a pleasant afternoon.''

Ferris looked startled, almost as though she wanted to ask how she could possibly do that in the job she had. But she just nodded.

Terry shifted the briefcase to her other hand and opened the door. The air outside was warm, but it was fresh. She pulled in a good lung full and wrinkled her nose. Whew! How could Toohey sit all day in that awful stench? She'd have to hang her suit on the porch overnight to air, to get that foul odor of cigar smoke out of it.

She started down the steps. Toohey was a prize, all right. If only they could get him off the Council. There were plenty of rumors about his dishonesty, but no proof. And he hadn't given her any today either. No proof, just hassle. And without proof no one could do a thing to—

Harrison stepped out from behind a pillar, matching his stride to hers. ''All finished?''

A Question of Trust   95

Why wasn't she surprised to see him? "Finally. The old windbag asks the same questions over and over. He's so infuriating I'd just like to explode. I spent half the time praying for patience and the other half trying to make him understand the simplest things."

Harrison nodded. "I know. Sometimes I think he's seen too many old movies. Thinks he's Humphrey Bogart or something."

She had to laugh. "He strikes me as more like Sydney Greenstreet."

"You're right." Harrison looked around with exaggerated care as though someone might be spying on them. "But don't tell him."

"Not me." She raised an eyebrow. "By the way, what are you doing here now?"

He grinned. "Would you believe me if I said I forgot something?"

She knew that sparkle in his eye. He was dangling the bait and when she bit— But she asked anyway. "Like what?"

"Like you."

That almost threw her. "Harrison, what are you talking about?"

He looked sheepish. "Well, to tell you the truth, I don't trust Toohey. I mean, you're a woman and—"

Some part of her was pleased, really pleased, that he wanted to protect her, but another part was

96   *Nina Coombs Pykare*

ticked off that he thought she *needed* protecting, couldn't take care of herself.

"I can take care of myself!" she cried. He couldn't know that most of her anger was put on.

He hesitated, then fell in step again. "I know. I just—"

"You shouldn't be standing around wasting the taxpayers' money."

"I wasn't wasting anything," he said defensively. He patted his own briefcase and pointed to the little park. "I sat on the bench over there and worked."

He looked directly into her eyes. "And anyway, you misunderstood what I meant. I knew you could handle Toohey."

"But you said you came back to—" She stopped. What *had* he said before she jumped to conclusions? *Uh-oh, I've done it again. Started judging.*

"I said I forgot something."

"Oh?"

"I forgot to ask you when we can have dinner again."

They had reached her car. Her heart pounding, she unlocked the door. "I don't know. Give me a call."

His grin said he wasn't fooled by her business-like attitude. "I will," he said, "you can bet on it. But I have to go out of town for a couple of days. I'll call you when I get back.'' And blowing her a kiss, he went off.

He can be such an infuriating man. She fastened her seat belt. *But I like the idea that he was concerned about me. I'm afraid I like it too much.*

Chapter Twelve

When Terry got home, the phone was ringing. She dropped the briefcase and ran for it. That crazy Harrison—calling her this soon! "Matthews Concrete," she said, kicking off her pumps and dropping into a chair. "Terry speaking."

"Oh, Terry, honey," her mom said. "I thought I'd have to leave a message. And you know I don't trust those awful machines."

So, it wasn't Harrison. That was all right. Terry swallowed. "Well, I'm here now, Mom. So, what is it?"

"It's my flight number, dear. I wanted to give it to you. I'll be getting in Thursday morning at eleven. Delta, Flight 732."

Terry grabbed a pencil and scribbled on the

A Question of Trust   99

message pad. "Fine, Mom, I'll be there when you get in."

"Thank you, dear. Terry, I—ah—I have a surprise for you."

"Mom, you know you don't have to bring me a present. Your coming to visit is enough of a gift."

"Yes, dear, but— Well, see you Thursday then."

"Yes, Mom, Thursday at eleven."

Terry put the receiver back and looked around. The place looked like a pigpen. Two days' dishes were piled in the sink. Clothes on the couch. Dust on everything. She'd have to clean house.

Mom came from that generation that really believed in the old adage, "cleanliness is next to godliness." Terry didn't. At least, not until she heard Mom was due for a visit. It was silly, of course, to go off on a frenzy of dusting and sweeping just because Mom was coming in.

But Mom didn't visit that often. And so when she did, Terry cleaned. She smiled. Actually, there was more to it than that. She didn't want to listen to Mom talk about poor housekeeping, or even worse, see Mom break out a bucket and sponge and start in scrubbing something.

Terry picked up her pumps and started up the stairs. Anyway, Mom's visits meant the place got a good cleaning once or twice a year.

100 *Nina Coombs Pykare*

And now, while her anger still burned at Toohey, now was the time to get at it. Anger created a lot of energy. Toohey had ruined her workday anyway, made it too late for her to go out to a job, too late to accomplish much of anything. Well, she'd use what was left of the day, and her anger, to whip this place into shape. With luck, she should be done by bedtime.

In the dream she was young again—five or so. Kris was eight, Sue seven. That Sunday afternoon they were supposed to be playing while the grown-ups visited. Kris dragged a lifesized baby doll by its left leg, bumping its head down the back steps. Sue had hers wrapped in a blanket, a *real* baby blanket, she kept saying.

And both of them treated Terry like dirt. She felt the tears swelling her throat, making it impossible to talk, stopping her from even asking, "Why? Why won't you let me play?"

Instead she said, "I have a baby doll." She held it out. "Her name's Marie."

The other two glared. "We don't want to play with you. You're too little. You're just a baby."

In the dream she held back the tears, held them back till she was alone, in the old grape arbor behind the house. There she hugged her doll to her, rocking in her pain. "I'm *not* a baby," she said, over and over. "I'm not. I'll show them."

A Question of Trust   101

In the dream the scene shifted. She was on the job with Dad, and Sue and Kris came by, pushing their doll carriages. "Ugh!" Sue said. "Such dirty stuff."

"Yuck!" Kris made a face. "How can you stand to touch it?"

But by then they didn't matter, by then Daddy was there—strong, comforting. He got down on his knee boards beside her. "Like this, honey, you do it like this. Thatta girl."

And in the dream she knew. When she grew up, she was going to be like Daddy. And he would smile at her and say, "Thatta girl."

She turned to face him. "I love you, Daddy. I love you so much!"

And in the dream, his rugged face lit with a smile. "You're gonna be the best concrete mason around."

She was happy and proud. Daddy loved her and—

She woke suddenly and lay there, smiling into the darkness. The dream wasn't new. She'd had it—or variations—many times. At first it had brought her to tears. But then, after a while, it had been comforting. Dad hadn't been much of a talker, but she'd never doubted that he loved her.

She rolled over and drifted off to sleep again. In this dream she was dressed for work, her tools in their bucket, her knee boards under her arm. She stood beside a pour so big she couldn't see the other side, so big it'd take at least two crews, maybe three. She looked around to tell them they'd better get started. And she was alone.

All alone—and facing what looked like miles of concrete already setting up.

Then Toohey was there. He came up out of the concrete like some malignant devil, and hovered over it, his gray silk suit running down into the concrete like little rivulets of dirty water. Cigar smoke hung over him in a smelly cloud and his little eyes blinked at her evilly. "Why? What? Where?" he thundered.

His questions all ran together, making no sense. "I can't talk now!" she cried. "The concrete's setting up. I've got to finish it."

Toohey swayed over her, a threatening gray blob. "You'll never make it," he said with a sneer. "Never make it. Never."

In the dream she was scared. Toohey could wipe out her business, put an end to her hopes. And he wanted to do that. She could see it in his eyes.

She wanted to run away, away from the evil in his face, but she couldn't leave the concrete. She had to finish the job.

She worked frantically, faster and faster. There was no end to it. She'd never be able to finish alone. And then she wasn't alone. Dad was work-

A Question of Trust 103

ing alongside her. "Don't worry, Terry," he said. "We'll make it."

"He's right."

She jerked around. Harrison! Harrison finishing concrete! He didn't know how to do that. At least she didn't think he did. "We'll make it," he said, blowing her a kiss.

And then she woke up.

Good grief! Dad and Harrison in the same dream. What did *that* mean?

Lying there, watching the sunrise through her window, she smiled. What would Harrison make of these dreams? He'd make something, of course, with his bent for psychoanalyzing.

She tried to remember. Had Kris and Sue really been that mean to her? And *had* that led to her fascination with her work? It was hard to say. But however it had happened, whatever had caused it, she loved working concrete.

The dream about the big pour wasn't so hard to understand. She'd been worrying about the municipal building ever since they got the bid. If a big job went wrong, it meant big trouble.

So her subconscious had tapped right into her fear and given her the big pour she couldn't finish alone. And then her subconscious had sent her some help. Dad she could understand. She dreamed of him often, and always his presence was healing, comforting. Just as it had been in real

104 *Nina Coombs Pykare*

life. So that was no surprise. It was almost like Dad himself was helping her through those dreams.

But why dreams about Harrison? The man probably didn't know a thing about finishing concrete. Why had he come to help her?

She stretched. *Wishful thinking, Matthews. You've been doing some wishful thinking. Time to get up and get to work.*

Chapter Thirteen

On Thursday morning, the rain fell in buckets. Terry looked out past the flashing wipers and frowned. She didn't want to greet Mom looking like a drowned rat. But maybe the rain would let up. She hoped so. Sunshine would be better. She knew rain was necessary, but sunshine was always better.

Cleveland International was crowded as always. By the time Terry reached the concourse, she had a terrific stitch in her side. Sidestepping slower-moving walkers, she looked ahead anxiously. She was usually early for everything, but Harrison's call had come just as she was leaving the house. She smiled, thinking how good his voice made her feel, how happy she'd been to know he'd be home

106 *Nina Coombs Pykare*

again tomorrow. He hadn't said just what time. But since it was tomorrow it would give her a chance to get Mom settled.

But now she had to find Mom. And she was late. She would still have had plenty of time to get to the airport, in spite of the call, if the state hadn't been fixing the turnpike. Miles of one-lane traffic had slowed everyone down. Of course, she shouldn't complain—highway repairs made work for concrete masons.

But Mom hated being alone in airports. She always had some friend take her there, a friend who'd promise to wait till the flight left. And she always wanted Terry there—waiting for her—when she got off the plane.

There it was. Finally. Gate 17. Now where was Mom? Ah, over there, talking to that tall thin man. Beside him, short, round Mom looked even shorter and rounder. But why was she talking to him? Mom was the shy type, hardly ever talked to strangers, and certainly not to strange men. Well, maybe he had something to do with the airport. Or maybe Mom had known him in Florida somehow.

Terry hurried up. ''Mom! Sorry I'm late. The turnpike was—''

''It's all right, honey.'' Theresa gave her a big hug.

Terry drew back. ''I was worried about you. I know you don't like being alone here and—''

A Question of Trust   107

"It's all right, Terry." Theresa's smile grew bigger. "I wasn't alone."

Terry looked at the man again. Tall and lanky with a shock of gray hair and a twinkle in his blue eyes, he looked harmless enough. "That's very kind of you, sir. Thanks. Come on, Mom, let's go get your luggage."

But her mom didn't move. "Terry, I—Terry, this is Tom Masters."

"I'm pleased to meet you, Mr. Masters, but Mom, we have to go. I've got an appointment later this afternoon."

Still her mom didn't move. Her face started to turn pink and her forehead wrinkled in the frown that meant she was really worried. "Terry, Terry honey, Tom is the surprise I told you about. He— We—we're married! He's my husband."

Husband? For a minute the breath left Terry's lungs. Had she heard right? "Married?" she stammered, staring from one to the other.

The man shook his head. "Really, Theresa, give the kid a break. That's not something to spring on her in a crowded airport. Didn't I tell you, you should have let her know beforehand?"

Theresa nodded, her round face serious. "I tried to, Tom, the last couple of times I called her. I tried to. I told you that. But I just couldn't do it. It just didn't seem right."

Terry opened her mouth to say, *And this is?*

But she closed it again without speaking. This couldn't be happening. It couldn't. *Mom married to a man I've never even heard of!*

How had this happened? When? But he was right about one thing—the concourse was no place to discuss anything.

"Let's go get the luggage," she said, wondering how she could sound so normal. She started down the concourse, Mom on her right, Tom beyond her.

"It happened real sudden," Mom said, in that soft voice she used when she was embarrassed.

"Sudden?" What did that mean?

Over Mom's head, Tom looked at Terry and chuckled. "Now, Terry, we didn't get drunk or anything, and run off. We'd been seeing each other for a while and we wanted to be together all the time. So we thought we'd get married. Seemed the right thing to do."

"We wanted you to be there," Mom went on, "but it's your busy season. I knew you couldn't get away and we didn't want to wait because— well—we're not getting any younger."

Her heart in her throat, Terry stopped right there, ignoring the people who streamed around them. "Mom! You're not sick! Oh, please, tell me you're not sick."

"No, no, honey. I'm fine." Mom put an arm around her. "It's just, well, some friends of ours,

A Question of Trust 109

they've been widowed, too, and they lead such lonely lives.''

She took Tom's arm and smiled up at him, at her husband. ''We didn't want to do that.''

Terry bit her bottom lip. She'd never expected to see that look of devotion on Mom's face again. Mom had never looked at anyone but Dad like that. And now—Terry blinked back the sudden tears.

''I'm sorry about the shock,'' Tom said. And she could tell he meant it. But it didn't make things any better. This was wrong. Mom married to another man was just wrong.

''How's the job going?'' Mom asked, starting to move on. ''The big one you wrote me about?''

''Oh, it's all right. The councilman's a pain, but we're managing.''

''And Pete and his wife?''

''They're fine.''

How could Mom go on like this—asking the usual questions, acting as though nothing had happened, as though everything was all right?

''Wasn't there a man connected to that job?'' Mom asked, her face lighting up.

Not now, Terry thought. *Not the marriage thing now.* She knew where Mom was headed with this, but she wasn't going. ''Takes a lot of men for a job this size.''

Mom chuckled. ''Now, Terry, you know that's

not what I mean. This man was the city manager. You went out to dinner with him that time.''

''A business dinner,'' Terry said. ''That's all—business.''

Tom smiled at her. ''You know your mama, Terry, she's a born matchmaker. Why, she's paired up half the folks in our trailer park already.''

Theresa blushed like a young girl. ''Now Tom, you know I just want to see everyone as happy as we are.''

Tom laughed. ''Truth to tell, darling, I don't think that's possible!''

They reached the luggage carousel, and Tom turned. ''Terry, maybe you'd like to go bring the car around. We can get the bags and meet you out front. If that's okay.''

She nodded. ''Sure.'' What difference did it make who picked up the bags? This stranger could carry them, this stranger Mom had married.

Well, she thought, hurrying along the moving walkway. *First things first.* She had to bring the car around. She had to take them both home. Mom would never forgive her if she didn't. But thank goodness, this wasn't the house she'd grown up in. Bringing this stranger to that house with all its wonderful family memories would have been too much.

* * *

A Question of Trust   111

Minutes later they were on the road. The car was too small. A ridiculous thought, Terry told herself, since even with the luggage there was room for six people. But still she couldn't help it—she felt trapped.

Mom was in the front seat. At least she hadn't climbed in back with *him,* the stranger who was her new husband. How could this have happened? How could Mom have forgotten all those wonderful years with Dad?

"Must have had a pretty heavy storm," Mom said, gazing out at the wet highway.

"Yes. It was a bad one."

"But it didn't affect our flight. Did it, Tom?"

"No, honey. The flight was real smooth."

Was that a slight emphasis on the word *flight*? Was he trying to hint that she was being rude? Well, maybe she was. But what about them? They could hardly expect her to jump with joy when something like this was sprung on her.

"Was it raining when you left home?" Mom asked. "Were you pouring concrete today?"

Terry nodded. "We were supposed to, but I imagine Pete canceled."

"I suppose so."

When lightning flashed in the distance and thunder rumbled, her mother flinched and shrank back against the seat. Tom leaned up to put a hand on her shoulder. "It's okay, honey."

His fingers were long and narrow, not short and blunt like Dad's. Dad's hands had been so strong, so capable.

Tom patted Mom's shoulder. "That storm's a long way off, Theresa. No need to worry."

Mom cast an apologetic look over her shoulder. "I know—it's silly of me. I should know better, but—"

"We all have our little fears," Terry said. "It's okay." That was dumb, spouting one of Dad's sayings! She bit her bottom lip. Mom would think she'd done it on purpose. That she was trying to be rude.

But Mom just smiled. "Win always said that. And he was right."

"Sounds like he was a good man."

"He was," Terry said, her voice husky. "A real good man."

Mom tried to make conversation, and Terry tried to answer. But it was hard enough to think about driving with her thoughts tumbling in circles. And making small talk at the same time was more than she could handle.

"I just believe I'll take a little nap," Tom said. "Be fresher for later, you know."

Mom turned to smile at him. "Okay, honey."

Terry tried to concentrate on the road. With the man right there in the backseat—even if he was sleeping—she couldn't ask the questions bouncing

A Question of Trust   113

around in her head. *Why? How could you? What will I do?*

Maybe it was just as well. If she could have gotten Mom alone, she might have lost it, might have sobbed out her feelings of grief and betrayal—and anger. She knew, on some level she knew, that Mom was a woman like other women, with a need for love and companionship. *I know it isn't fair to expect anyone to go on alone indefinitely.*

But this is my mother. And to just be told, like some two-year-old, that her mother was already married—well, it was hard to swallow.

"I'm more tired than I thought," Mom said into the silence. "Guess I'll doze, too."

"Sure." Terry tried to keep the hurt out of her voice. If *he* wasn't there, they'd be chattering away, a mile a minute, filling each other in on every little detail since the last time they'd been together. She'd always looked forward to these times, to the sharing of their thoughts. Now that was gone, too.

It wasn't fair. Death had taken Dad—and now this stranger had taken Mom. Terry swallowed the lump of tears in her throat. *It isn't fair at all.*

When they pulled in the driveway in midafternoon, Terry woke Mom, then went around to open the back. She'd have to get more groceries later.

It irked her that this man would sit down at the table with them, but really what else could she do?

"Here," Tom said, lifting out the suitcases. "I'll carry these." His eyes twinkled down at her. "I know you can do it, but I've got to admit I'm from the older generation. I just believe some things are man's work."

She was too tired to argue with him. And anyway, what else could she expect? This man wasn't like Dad at all. How could Mom love him?

Terry was turning away from the rear of the wagon when a car pulled in the drive. Harrison's car. Her heart skipped a beat. What was he doing here? He wasn't supposed to be back till tomorrow. She wanted to see him, but not now, not in front of Mom. Mom was sure to say something embarrassing. And the day was already a disaster.

"Nice machine," Tom said, eyeing the Mercedes as it came to a stop behind them. "Real nice."

Smiling, Harrison climbed out and came toward her. "Terry, darling!" Ignoring the others, he swept her into his arms for a throbbing kiss.

When he released her mouth, her knees were weak and her fists were clenched. It wasn't bad enough she had to deal with this new husband of Mom's; now Harrison was back too soon. And his stupid kiss—much as she'd enjoyed it—would have Mom giving her the third degree. "I thought you weren't getting back till tomorrow."

A Question of Trust   115

His arms still around her, Harrison smiled down into her face. "I finished early, and I couldn't wait to get home. Sweetheart, it's sure good to see you. But tell me, who's this?"

Before she could answer, Mom smiled and said, "I'm Terry's mother."

"Mrs. Matthews." Harrison took her hand.

"No, Mrs. Masters."

When Harrison looked confused, Tom stepped forward and extended his hand. "Name's Tom. Tom Masters. We just got married, Theresa and me," he explained. "Shortly 'fore we came up here. Sort of took Terry by surprise, I'm afraid. Theresa was gonna tell her 'fore we got here, but she couldn't quite manage it."

"I see." Looking a little dazed, Harrison shook Tom's hand, but his gaze went to Terry. His eyes said he was sorry, said he understood.

"Listen, honey," he said. "I just got back. Haven't even been home yet. What say we go to dinner tonight? All of us. Say about seven? That'll give me a little while to see what's on my desk and freshen up. My treat, of course."

"Oh, we can't let you do that," Theresa said, beaming. "It's too much."

Terry didn't like the way Mom was looking at him, like a cat with a saucer of cream.

"No trouble, Mrs. Masters. Terry's family, well, they're important to me." He glanced toward her.

"She's really something. Has she told you about the big municipal job yet?"

"A little," Theresa said, her smile growing bigger. "Not much."

Harrison grinned. "That's okay. She can tell you all about it over dinner."

Finally Terry found her tongue. "I have an appointment at five and—"

"We'll wait on you." He squeezed her waist. "I'm sure your folks won't mind." He turned his smile on them all. "You see, I've been out of town for three whole days and I missed her something awful."

Tom chuckled. "We understand. We'd be pleased to go to dinner, but we'll pay our own way. It's better like that."

Harrison kissed her once more, a kiss that left her with knees like limp spaghetti and, when she got a look at her mother's face, made her feel like strangling him. Then he grinned and drove away.

"So that's the man," her mom said before the car was all the way out the driveway.

Terry whirled. "Now, Mom, don't start! Don't pay any attention to Harrison. He gets carried away."

Theresa laughed. "I saw the way he looked at you, honey. I'd say there's going to be another wedding in the family soon."

"Mom! Please! Forget it." What lousy timing.

A Question of Trust 117

I can't tell Mom my suspicions about Harrison. But if I let her think—

"He's the one, honey. I feel it in my bones."

Terry sighed. There was no point in trying to convince her mom that Harrison was only a business acquaintance. He'd made sure of that. But she had to say or do something. "It's too soon, Mom. Everything's happening too fast."

"Come on, you two," Tom called from the porch. "You can gab later. These bags are heavy."

Chapter Fourteen

The restaurant was crowded when they got there at eight, but the maître d' took one look at Harrison and led them immediately to a table. Her mother's knowing look didn't improve Terry's mood. It had been a long, difficult day, climaxed by a meeting with a client who'd obviously decided against giving her the job long before he heard the quote. And this dinner wasn't going to improve things. But she could at least be polite. That much could be expected from her at least.

"Nice place," Tom said, looking around.

Harrison nodded. "We like it."

She shot him a hard look. What did he mean, *we*? They'd only been there twice. And saying *we*

118

A Question of Trust

in that tone of voice was bound to give Mom ideas—the wrong kind of ideas.

"We like the swordfish."

What was he up to? One more *we* like that and she was going to kick him under the table. Good and hard. *Sorry, but he's just so aggravating!*

"Actually," she said, "I like the salmon better."

Tom sent her mother a look and Mom sighed. "So Terry, tell me about the municipal job."

Terry shrugged. She'd rather not talk about it at all, rather not think about the trouble on this job. But she knew Mom. "There's not that much to tell," she said. "It's a big job. And the councilman's a pain."

Tom frowned. "How big a job?"

"The biggest we've ever had." She wanted her words to sound thrilled, but somehow they came out sounding worried.

Mom frowned. "Nothing can go wrong, can it?"

Terry forced a little laugh. "Of course, it can, Mom. Something can always go wrong. But we'll manage. We're fine." It was a lie. All a lie. If they blew this job, Matthews Concrete could go down the tubes. But she didn't want to talk about that. She didn't even want to think about it.

Mom was staring at her, her expression concerned. Any minute now she'd start in with the questions. *Not tonight,* Terry prayed. *Please, not tonight.* She didn't think she could take much more.

"I wouldn't worry," Harrison said. "I'm sure Terry can handle anything that might happen. She's very competent."

Tom nodded. "I can see that already. This councilman—what's he like?"

"A windbag," Terry said. "And always asking stupid questions. Always."

Mom frowned. "Doesn't sound like a nice man to deal with."

For the first time since she'd heard of the marriage, Terry laughed. "That's the understatement of the year, Mom. But Harrison's right; I'll deal with Toohey."

That seemed to convince Mom. She nodded, then threw Harrison an arch look. She really was taken with the man. "Nice music they play here. Do you dance, Mr. Green?"

"Oh, yes. It's one of the reasons we come here. But do call me Harrison." He turned to Terry. "If your mother will order for us, maybe we can squeeze in a dance before the food comes."

"Sure thing," Tom said. "What do you want?"

"Just tell them the swordfish and rice pilaf."

Harrison got to his feet and took her by the hand. Terry went, but she wasn't sure whether she

A Question of Trust

wanted to dance with him or stomp on his toes. *I'm doing it again. That old temper of mine.*

"I wanted salmon," she said, as he swung her into his arms.

"Sorry." He didn't look sorry. He looked pleased, his eyes sparkling. "I ordered swordfish out of deference to your mother. But I can change it."

"Never mind." She looked up at him. "You can do something else for me, though."

He smiled. "Anything. Just name it."

She doubted that. "Quit trying to convince my mother that we're the perfect couple. She's an incurable romantic and she wants me to mar—to settle down."

He nodded. "Most mothers want their daughters to settle down. Nothing wrong with that."

"There is when a mother keeps pounding it in, keeps telling her daughter that time's passing, life's passing."

He looked down at her, his eyes sober. "Maybe she's right."

She couldn't buy that. "Maybe she is. And maybe she isn't. But it's my life."

"You're right about that," he said. "Dead right. But I don't think there's any sense in trying to hide the truth."

She had to bite. "And what truth is that?"

"Your mother's no dummy. She knows if a big job goes bad, it can wipe out a whole company."

"We're all right," she insisted. "We'll make it." They had to.

He pulled her a little closer, resting his chin on her hair. "I'm sure you will."

They danced in silence for a few minutes. Then Harrison said, "Why don't you like him?"

"Who? Toohey? He's—"

"Not Toohey. You know I don't mean him." His voice was gently teasing. "Why don't you like Tom?"

"I never said I don't like him."

"You don't have to *say* it," Harrison went on. "It's written all over you."

"How can you say that? Just because you like to play shrink and—"

He gathered her closer. "I'm not playing shrink, honey. Any fool with eyes can see how you feel about Tom. I just wondered why."

Am I really that transparent? I don't want to hurt Tom's feelings, but . . . "You're the one with all the theories," she said. "You tell me."

"Well, since he seems like a nice enough guy, and it's easy to see your mother loves him, I'd guess it's because you're jealous."

"I am not!"

"You probably never thought your mother

A Question of Trust   123

would marry again," he went on, as though she hadn't spoken.

"You got that right!"

"Do you think that's fair? Your mother's got a lot of years left. Do you really want her to live them alone?"

"Of course I don't. But—"

"But Tom isn't your father."

Maybe he's right. But it hurts. It hurts so much. I miss Dad, and . . . "I don't want to talk about it," she said. "Please."

"Okay. Sure."

He gave in too easily; he must be plotting a new strategy. To stop him she said the first thing that came into her head.

"Have you ever done any concrete work?" Good grief, what a completely stupid thing to ask.

"No, afraid not." He looked down at her. "Why?"

"Nothing, I—"

He shook his head. "Terry, Terry, you should never lie. You do it so badly. Your face gives you away."

He was probably right about that, too. She didn't usually lie and she wasn't good at it. "Okay, okay. I just thought you might know how. I had a dream, that's all, and you were in it."

His eyebrows went up. "Me?"

"Yes, we were working. That is, *I* was working.

Biggest pour I've ever seen. And I was alone. Then Toohey came up out of the wet concrete like some horrible genie and hovered there, glowering and telling me I'd never make it.''

''And then I was there.'' Harrison's grin widened. ''Your knight in shining armor, trowel in hand.''

She grinned back. ''Well, first my dad was there. Then you. And the three of us were working like crazy. So I just thought, maybe—''

''Sorry. I don't know a thing about concrete. But I think I'm going to learn.''

''Why?''

His eyes sparkled at her. ''I'll give you three guesses. The first two don't count.''

The dance ended, and they turned back to the table. Why should he want to learn about concrete? It didn't make sense. Why would a man like Harrison want to dirty his hands? Unless— She pushed the thought aside. He couldn't be doing it because Toohey wanted him to, to find something wrong with her work. He couldn't, but . . .

Back at the table, her mother and Tom were holding hands like teenagers. ''We ordered your swordfish,'' Tom said.

''Thanks.'' Harrison held her chair for her.

Terry could feel Mom looking her over. Nothing would escape her inspection. Tomorrow Terry

A Question of Trust 125

would hear every detail, from her flushed cheeks to the supposed look of love in her eyes.

To avoid a comment right then, she asked, ''So what have you two been talking about?'' She'd show Harrison he was wrong. She wasn't jealous of Tom. She was just . . .

''Been talking about politicians.'' Tom sent an apologetic look in Harrison's direction. ''Not you, son. We agree as to city managers being honest and aboveboard.'' He grinned. ''For the most part.''

''What we don't agree on,'' Mom said with a smile, ''is politicians.''

Terry leaned forward, wanting to know more. Maybe if they disagreed about enough things . . . But Mom looked so happy. ''What about politicians?'' Terry asked.

''Your mother says they're a fact of life and you gotta deal with 'em. I say you don't. Ought to be able to make a decent living without having to go anywhere near 'em.''

''You're right,'' Terry said. ''They're self-serving, many of them, out for what they can get. They never give straight answers. And half the time they don't know what they're talking about.''

Tom grinned. ''Bet your dad didn't like to deal with 'em, either.''

''You're right, he didn't. Maybe I shouldn't have tried for the municipal job. But people kept

126 *Nina Coombs Pykare*

after me to make a bid. And it seemed like the thing to do.''

Tom nodded. ''I'm sure it'll work out all right.''

''Sure.'' She wasn't sure, of course, but she tried to inject belief into her voice. No use worrying Mom. ''Say, how do you know so much about politicians?''

Tom smiled. ''I was a plumber before I retired. Did a job for the city once—when I was a young man, still wet behind the ears. Crooked politician almost ruined me. Never touched another city job. Promised myself I wouldn't touch anything that even might be crooked.''

Crooked. Crooked. The word bounced around in her head till she wanted to scream.

''Crooked politicians can make a lot of trouble,'' Harrison agreed politely. ''But lucky for us here in Stonybrook, our elected officials are above reproach.''

Terry stared at him, biting back the words that rushed to her lips. How could he say such a thing? He knew the rumors about Toohey. He had to. Why was he denying them? Was he trying to cover up?

She could tell from Tom's expression that he wasn't convinced either. The man was too smart for that.

The swordfish came then, and conversation fell off as they settled into eating. Catching Harrison's

A Question of Trust

gaze on her, she flushed a little. She could almost see the gears whirring in his head, see him thinking he was right, that she was jealous. *But he doesn't understand.*

Tom wasn't Dad. No one could take Dad's place. But looking across the table at her mother's glowing face, she had to admit—Mom really did look happy.

Chapter Fifteen

The next morning Terry got up even earlier than usual and left the house before the others came downstairs. Mom knew where everything was and would make her own breakfast as a matter of course. Tom's, too. And right now Terry didn't want to field a bunch of questions. She wanted to concentrate on work, not on Mom's imaginings about Harrison—or the wedding she probably had already planned completely!

Frowning, Terry dumped her lunch in the van. She didn't want to think about Harrison today. They were pouring at the municipal building again and she wanted to be there, to make sure everything went like it should.

As usual she was the first at the site. She wan-

A Question of Trust 129

dered around, looking things over, pulling in great gulps of construction-filled air. Maybe she was silly, but the smells of a site—the woodsy lumber, the acrid steel, and especially the odor of fresh concrete—they were all good smells to her, familiar, comforting smells that meant good things, sweet memories.

She squatted to inspect a form they'd set yesterday. On the job she always felt close to Dad. Oh, there was a stone in the cemetery, and she took flowers there. But it was here, on the job, with concrete to work, that she felt Dad's presence the most. Here she could almost forget he was gone. Here sometimes she thought she could turn and see him coming toward her, his knee boards under his arm, a smile on his rugged face.

Tears rose to her eyes and she reached out to touch the form, whispering, ''Oh, Dad, I wish you were here. I miss you so much.''

The sound of a car pulling into the lot brought her to her feet. She couldn't let Pete see her crying. Blinking the tears away, she turned. But this wasn't Pete. The sun was behind him, but that didn't matter; even in those clothes, she'd know him anywhere. ''Harrison, what are you doing here?''

He came toward her, grinning widely. ''I've come for my lessons, of course. I'm a man of my word.''

130   *Nina Coombs Pykare*

She stared at him, her heart pounding. "Lessons? Harrison, I—"

"I know concrete masons usually belong to the union, but I don't expect to get paid." He grinned. "At least not right off."

"Harrison, be sensible. I can't teach you this work. It takes time to learn everything, and—"

He looked down at his clothes—ragged jeans, a torn T-shirt, stout work shoes. "What's the matter? Didn't I dress right?"

"There's nothing wrong with your clothes, Harrison." They were great-looking clothes—for concrete work. And his body looked great, too. His arms were bare, fine dark hair curled over them, and, though he'd never finished concrete, it was clear he was in good shape. Very good shape. "It's more than a matter of clothes."

He nodded in agreement. "Of course it is." He put on a mock frown. "Say, you don't think I'm too dumb to learn—"

She had to laugh. "Of course not."

"That's good." He chuckled. "Because I like to think I'm smart enough to learn anything a five-year-old can learn."

She shook her head. "But I didn't learn it all at once. It took me years."

He shrugged. "So? I have plenty of time." He moved closer, grasping her elbows, making her want to lean into him. "Come on. Give me a

A Question of Trust   131

chance. Let me follow you around. Teach me a little bit at a time. I'm a fast learner. Honest.'' He bent to kiss the tip of her nose.

She pulled back and looked around wildly. She'd had a rough time living down their fall into the concrete and the kiss that followed. ''Harrison! Not here! The crew—''

''It's all right, boss lady. There's no one here to see.''

When she frowned at him, he said, ''Okay, okay,'' and dropped his hands from her elbows. ''I promise not to touch you''—perversely, her heart fell—''during working hours''—and rose again. ''I'll try not to ask stupid questions. But honest, I really do want to learn the business.''

The question burned in her heart. She might as well ask it. ''Why, Harrison? I want to know why.''

His face was sober. ''You can't guess?''

''No.'' All she could think about was Toohey, that this was some plan of Toohey's.

''I think it's too soon to tell you.'' Harrison's voice grew deeper, huskier. ''I don't want to scare you off.''

Now what did he mean by that? Was she really supposed to think that he loved her so much he wanted to learn her business? That was carrying love a little too far. Besides, he'd never *said* he loved her.

132   *Nina Coombs Pykare*

"Please," he repeated. "I promise to be good."

But what if he *did* mean that? What if he *did* love her that much? And besides, she wanted to do it, she wanted to see him dirty and sweaty, on his knees working concrete. But still—

" 'Morning, Terry," Pete said from behind her. " 'Morning there, Mr. Green."

She swung around, almost laughing out loud at Pete's wide-eyed startled look. " 'Morning, Pete."

Harrison nodded, but remained silent, his eyes fixed on her. She pulled in a deep breath and knew what she was going to do.

"Well, Pete, looks like we've got a new man on the crew. Issue Mr. Green a hard hat. He's going to be learning the trade."

Pete stared at her like she'd lost her mind—and maybe she had. But she was still going to do this.

Pete stood there, his mouth hanging open. "A hard hat," she repeated. "He's going to need it."

He shook himself. "Yeah, Terry. Sure, Terry." And off he went.

"Afraid you gave poor Pete a shock," Harrison said, grinning down at her.

Terry grinned back. "He'll get over it."

When Terry pulled into her driveway late that afternoon, all she wanted was a hot shower and her bed. It had been a long hard day. But having Harrison tag around after her hadn't been so bad—

A Question of Trust 133

after she got used to ignoring the raised eyebrows. He hadn't asked many questions, either, and the ones he had asked had made good sense.

Not much chance of getting to relax tonight. Mom'll have dinner ready, all my favorites probably. And I'll have to make polite conversation with Tom.

She climbed out of the van, gathered up her thermos and empty lunch bag, and made a face. Might as well get it over with. Mom would be in high gear, full of questions.

Terry pushed open the back door and sniffed. It couldn't be, but it was—turkey and dressing. "Mom, what on earth are you doing?"

Mom turned from the sink, potato in one hand, peeler in the other. "We don't get to be together on the holidays much anymore, so I thought I'd just fix a nice turkey dinner. I hope you don't mind."

"Mind? Of course not." She set her bucket and thermos on the counter. Was this a peace offering? "My mouth's watering already. But it's so much work."

Mom grinned. "Well, there wasn't much else to do. The house looks real nice. You must have just cleaned it."

Terry had to laugh. "I did. In honor of your coming."

Mom nodded. "I appreciate it, honey. But I suspect you'll be wanting to clean house more often now.''

''I will?'' For a minute Terry didn't make any connection. ''Why?''

Mom giggled. ''He's a fine-looking man, your Harrison. A good man, I think. And I can't see him living in a messy place. Not a man like that.''

''Oh, Mom, he's not *my* Harrison. I told you. I can't think about things like that yet. I'm not ready. It's too soon.''

Mom went back to peeling potatoes, her back stiff. ''Maybe it is, maybe it isn't. But I've a feeling Mr. Green's more than ready. The way he looks at you, the way he kisses you.'' She sighed. ''It's as plain as the nose on his face. The man's got it bad.''

Terry knew the blood was rushing to her cheeks, but instead of protesting any more, she asked, ''What can I do to help with dinner?''

''Just go get your shower, honey. I sent Tom to the store to get some good rolls. Didn't want to get into baking today.''

Terry started for the stairs.

Mom turned again. ''Terry, honey?''

Terry stopped. ''Yes?''

''About Tom. I know I should have called you before. I just—''

Terry stood there. She wanted to cross the kitchen and throw her arms around her mother, but

A Question of Trust   135

she couldn't. It was too hard. "It hurt, Mom. It hurt a lot. I mean, you and Dad were so good together. I just don't see how you could . . ."

Tears appeared in Mom's eyes. "I know it's hard for you to understand. But I've been so lonesome, honey. I missed your father so much. And Tom was missing his wife. And, well—it seemed like we were being given another chance at happiness. And we figured we ought to take it."

Terry wanted to say something comforting, but the pain was too sharp, too new. No words of forgiveness would come. That was probably what she should do—forgive. But she couldn't, not yet.

"I won't ever stop loving your father," Mom went on. "Tom knows that." She sniffled. "But I just couldn't stand being alone. I love Tom, too. It's just different."

Terry nodded. She was going to cry herself if she wasn't careful. "I'd better go get my shower."

Mom nodded and wiped her eyes on her apron. "Run along, honey. And—I love you."

"I love you, too." She could say that, even if she couldn't voice the words of forgiveness Mom wanted.

When Terry came down later, showered and changed into slacks and a cool top, she'd promised herself to make the best of things. She might be hurt, she *was* hurt, but Mom was married. So she would do the best she could to accept it.

"Hello, there," Tom said when she came into the kitchen. "Isn't this mother of yours something, though? Best cook I've ever seen."

"Oh, Tom. How you do go on!" Mom blushed like a young girl. "Now, Terry, we've set the table out here. It'll make cleanup easier." She glanced at the stove. "Everything's ready. So just sit down."

"I thought maybe Terry's fellow would be here," Tom said. "Nice man. I like him."

"I called his office," Mom said, sending her a worried look. "But his secretary said he couldn't be reached. I'm sorry, Terry."

How many times did she have to repeat this? "Mom, I told you. He's just a business acquaintance and—"

Tom frowned. "Mighty funny way to treat a business acquaintance. All that kissing and dancing."

"Tom's right," Mom said with a knowing smile. "Anyone can see how Harrison feels about you. And I think you feel the same way about him."

Terry stared down at her empty plate. If only she could tell them the truth, could tell them that Harrison might be into graft. But she didn't dare. Mom wasn't a good liar, and Tom—well, she

A Question of Trust   137

didn't know enough about Tom to trust him with her mother. And if either of them let something slip to Harrison, it could be disastrous. If he was Toohey's man—*but he couldn't be*, her heart said, *he just couldn't be*—she didn't want him to have any suspicions that she was on to him.

"I've told you, Mom. It's too soon for me to make any plans about Harrison." She turned to Tom. "And he's *not* my fellow."

"But he said—"

"I don't *care* what he said," she snapped. "Why won't anyone listen to me?"

"Now, now, honey." Mom leaned over to pat her hand. "You're just tired and hungry. Let's forget all about Harrison and enjoy our dinner."

And that, thought Terry, was the best idea anyone had had all day.

Chapter Sixteen

The dinner was delicious—and Terry did enjoy it. But when they were finished, she got to her feet. "If you'll just put the food away, Mom, I'll clean up when I get back."

"Do you have to go out again?" Theresa asked, disappointment in her voice. "We've hardly had a chance to talk."

"Sorry," Terry said. *I need to get away, to get some breathing space. I can only take so much of Tom and Mom gazing into each other's eyes like sappy teenagers.*

She turned at the door. "I shouldn't be too long. Might take a drive over to the municipal site."

Her mom looked worried. "Honey, you can't work all the time."

A Question of Trust   139

"I know, Mom, but this is a big job. An important job."

"Let the child go," Tom said, wrapping an arm around Theresa's waist. "She's a conscientious worker."

"But Tom—"

He kissed her cheek. "No buts now, Theresa. Terry's got work to do."

"That's right," Terry said. "See you later." And grabbing her purse and keys, she hurried out.

But before she could get down the back steps, the wind whipped her hair around her face, almost blinding her. She looked up. The sky shouldn't be this dark. It wasn't even seven yet. Looked like a storm coming, a bad one. Pete was going to be ticked off at the weathermen again. They'd promised no rain for the rest of the week.

She backed the van out the drive. Better get over to the municipal building and cover today's pour. The way the wind was freshening, this storm was coming soon. Lucky she kept that roll of plastic in the back of the van.

She cast another worried look at the sky. It was getting darker—wind whipping branches around. She'd be lucky to get there before the rain let loose. It wasn't going to be any picnic handling the plastic alone, either. Oh well, it wouldn't be the first time—or the last—that she'd wrestled plastic by herself.

140   *Nina Coombs Pykare*

By the time she pulled into the site parking lot, the blackness had spread from one side of the sky to the other. The place looked strange, eerie, lightning flashing over the metal skeleton of the building like some end-of-the-world movie.

But she couldn't waste time looking. She ran around to the back of the van and opened the door, wrestling with the roll of plastic. The wind whipped her hair into her eyes. Should have brought a scarf. There must be one somewhere in the van, but she didn't have time to look. The rain was coming any minute.

Pushing and pulling, she got the roll of plastic to the edge, and tipped it up over her shoulder. The wind grabbed at it, almost knocking her over. But she hefted it higher, slammed the door shut, and staggered off toward the concrete.

The wind was getting even stronger. She dumped the plastic to one side of a form and struggled to unroll a piece. It was rough, with the wind blowing like it was, working against her.

"Need some help?" He tapped her shoulder.

"Harrison!" she yelled. "Oh, yes. We've got to get this covered."

The wind took the words out of her mouth, but he seemed to understand. He grabbed one end of the plastic and helped her pull out a length. She cut it across. Struggling against the wind, they unfolded it. Harrison took one end and hurried to the

A Question of Trust   141

other side of the concrete. The wind caught the plastic, almost tearing it out of her hands, but she held on. They worked fast, against time and the rising wind. And finally they had it stretched over the pour.

"Now what?" he asked during a lull in the wind.

"We push it against the wet concrete," she called. "Not hard. Just a little!"

He looked surprised, but he did what she said. And as always the wet concrete sucked it down.

And just in time, too, because then the rain came pelting down, great heavy drops soaking through to their skins. Harrison's jeans and shirt clung to him, his dark hair was plastered to his head, and rain dripped from his nose. She probably didn't look any better.

A deafening clap of thunder nearly broke her eardrums and lightning sizzled down through the exposed girders of the building.

"Too close!" Harrison yelled, pulling her into his arms. She clung to him as another bolt of lightning streaked the sky.

"The trailer!" she cried. "We can wait it out in there."

Hand in hand, they ran for it. She pulled out her key ring and unlocked the door. Another crash of thunder sent them scurrying inside. She flipped the

142 *Nina Coombs Pykare*

light switch, but the trailer remained dark. ''Power must be out.''

Harrison turned from closing the door. ''Flashlights?''

Terry laughed. ''I left mine in the van.'' She shivered. That rain had been cold. ''What about you?''

''Left mine in the car.''

''Then I guess we'll have t-to wait it out in the d-dark. Just wish we had some d-dry clothes.''

Lightning flashed. The trailer was dim, but she could see his silhouette.

''Honey, you're shivering.''

''I'll be all right. It's just being wet and—''

Lightning flashed again and he was right there, in front of her. ''I'm all wet, too,'' he said. ''Listen, didn't I see an old leather couch in here?''

''Yes.''

''Then come on. We'll sit there and warm each other up.''

She wasn't sure that was such a good idea, but she couldn't afford to get sick—and going out in a storm like this was really stupid. They could be struck by lightning. So she let him take her hand and lead her to the couch.

The arm he put around her, though wet, was warm, and she snuggled against him gratefully. ''Now,'' she said, ''you see why you don't want to get into this business.''

A Question of Trust 143

In the dimness, he chuckled. "Oh, I don't know. Seems kind of exciting to me."

Come to think of it, what was he doing around here anyway? He lived clear on the other side of town. "By the way, what are you doing here?"

"I was coming over to your place, and—"

"My place? Why?"

"Your mother left a message on my machine— turkey dinner and all the trimmings. I didn't hear it right away because I went straight to the shower and didn't listen to my messages till after. But I haven't had a good turkey dinner for ages and I figured your mother made plenty—so I was coming to see about the leftovers."

She looked up. "But then why did you come *here?*"

All she could see was his eyes, gleaming in the darkness.

"One day I heard you and Pete talking about covering pours. And later I asked someone what happened if it rained." The arm around her tightened. "And knowing you, I figured you'd be here to cover it. I thought maybe Pete'd be here, too, but—"

"He went out of town for a wedding. Left right after work."

"Then it's a good thing I came."

"A very good thing." She lowered her cheek

144   *Nina Coombs Pykare*

against his shirt, feeling his warmth, hearing the steady beating of his heart under her ear.

There was silence between them for a few minutes, but it was good silence.

Then Harrison said, "Terry, I want to talk to you about something."

Comfortable there against his chest, she murmured, "Go ahead."

"Honey, I think you know this. I'm sure your mother does."

She lifted her head in surprise. "My mother?" Why did her voice have to squeak like that?

He frowned. "I'm making a mess of this. What I'm trying to say—I'm falling in love with you."

There, there were the words she wanted to hear!

"But I'm not at all sure how you feel about me," he went on. "And I want to be sure. Terry, do you love me?"

All the breath seemed to leave her body and she struggled to think what to say. Why was he telling her this now?

"I—I think so." She *knew* so, but she couldn't tell him just yet, not till this job was done and she could be absolutely sure he wasn't involved in any graft.

He sighed. "Well, I guess that's better than a definite no."

She turned in his arms and reached up to touch his cheek. "I care about you, Harrison. I care

A Question of Trust   145

about you more than I've ever cared about any man.''

In the dim light she saw him raise a dark eyebrow. ''More than you cared about Jeff?''

So he knew about Jeff. She didn't hesitate. ''Yes, much more.''

''And you were going to marry him. Right?''

''Yes.''

''And you care more for me?''

''Yes, but—''

He put a finger across her lips. ''Stop there, honey. I'll give you time—all the time you need. I just wanted to know if I have a chance.''

She smiled up at him. ''You do, Harrison. It's just that it's too soon. And I want to be sure. I almost made an awful mistake with Jeff. So now I want to be more careful. You can understand that.''

''I can understand it,'' he grumbled tenderly, ''but I don't like it.''

''Give me—give me till the municipal job is done. Okay?''

''I suppose it'll have to be.'' He put a hand under her chin and tipped her face up to his. ''But I'll need a lot of kisses to help me make it, and—''

The honking of a car horn jerked them apart. ''Who—?'' she cried, jumping to her feet and rushing to the window. ''It's the company truck. And it's stopped raining.''

146 *Nina Coombs Pykare*

Harrison looked surprised. "So it has. But if Pete's gone, who—"

"It's Mom!" Terry threw open the door and hurried out, splashing through puddles. "Mom, what are you doing here?"

Instead of answering, Theresa flung her arms around her. "Terry, you're soaking wet! You *were* caught in the storm."

"I came to cover the concrete, and—"

"Hello, Harrison," Tom said, climbing out of the truck. "Looks like you got rained on, too."

Harrison stepped down from the trailer. "We'd just managed to get the plastic down when the storm broke. The lightning was real close, so we decided to wait it out in the trailer."

"Of course," Mom said. "Oh, Terry, honey, I was so worried. You out in that storm, and—"

"I'm all right, Mom." She patted Theresa's arm and smiled encouragingly. "Listen, Harrison got your message about dinner late. He was on his way to the house for leftover turkey."

Mom's smile practically lit up the parking lot. "You just come right along, Harrison. We've got plenty."

Tom helped her mother back into the truck, then turned to Terry. "Never would have thought she'd budge in a storm like that. Not the way she is about storms." He shook his head. "And there she was running right out into the rain to get to the truck

A Question of Trust 147

and come looking for you.'' He hesitated. ''Hope it was all right to take the truck.''

''Of course.''

Tom looked at Theresa with pride. ''She's sure some woman.''

''You're right, Tom,'' Terry said, surprising herself by grinning at him. ''Aren't we lucky to have her? Come on. I've worked up an appetite again. Let's get back to that turkey.''

Chapter Seventeen

Toward noon on the Thursday following the storm, Terry put down her pen, leaned back in her chair, and sighed. The office seemed so quiet, so empty. There was a lot more paperwork to do, but she had already done a lot. Maybe if she took a break— She tipped her chair back, put her feet up on the desk. In just these few days she'd gotten used to Harrison being right there, to having him behind her when she turned. He worked hard and seemed to enjoy it. She'd been spending more time on the job sites so she could show him how to do things with concrete—to set a form, to straight-edge and bull float, and to achieve that last smooth finish that customers wanted.

Having Harrison go to work with her made her

A Question of Trust   149

feel good, made her feel alive. Of course, she still didn't know any more about the rumors of graft. She knew there was something not right about Toohey, though. Even before the rumors started, she'd felt that in her bones. But whatever Toohey was doing, Harrison had nothing to do with it, knew nothing about it. He just couldn't. She had to believe that.

She looked up at the big Mickey Mouse clock on the wall. Eleven-fifteen. Last night she'd told Harrison she might stop by the municipal building around noon. Probably she was being paranoid about this job, but she couldn't help being nervous about a bid that could ruin her company. And being on-site and seeing how things were going there made her feel better. Anyway, that was just normal business procedure.

She got up and stretched. The municipal job would be finished eventually. And when it was, she would know what answer she was going to give Harrison. A Christmas wedding might be nice. If they could wait that long.

Don't go counting your chickens before they're hatched, she warned herself with a laugh. *Get the job done first. And make sure he's not . . .*

Grabbing her keys and hard hat, she headed for the station wagon.

*   *   *

150   *Nina Coombs Pykare*

The building site was a madhouse of activity. Three different crews were working there. Off to one side, a man was shoulder deep in a hole, throwing out dirt. "Hi, Terry," he called.

"Hi, Kenny," she called back.

Funny, she didn't remember anything going in at that spot, but then, she usually only remembered the work her own crews were doing. And Kenny worked for Do-It Construction, not for her.

She skirted a pile of lumber. Might as well have another look at that pour they'd covered last week, then she could check the other things.

The concrete looked fine. They'd taken the plastic off the next day, of course. And the concrete had cured just like it should. She sighed. This was a big job and it paid well, but she wished she hadn't taken it. She just didn't feel good about it. Those rumors of graft, and—

"Cave-in!"

The shout sucked the air from her lungs. Kenny! She whirled and raced back the way she'd come. The hole was full of dirt and Kenny had disappeared beneath it.

Buried! Kenny was in there, buried alive. "Get some boards over here" she cried. "Quick! Keep these sides from giving way any more. I'm going down."

"You can't—"

But she was already in the hole, throwing out

A Question of Trust

dirt with her hard hat. The dirt was loose and sandy, but that meant it kept shifting, sliding down, down. Kenny couldn't last long in there. He had to have air. And the weight of the dirt would soon crush him. Thank heavens the hole wasn't too big. She scooped dirt to one side, away from where she'd last seen him. She could move it easily, but it kept pouring back toward the center. She plunged her hand in as far as it would go. She had to find him, to get him—

There! Her fingers had hit something. His arm! She scooped more dirt away, following the arm down to his chest—and finally she reached his head. Evidently, the dirt had knocked him backward and he'd thrown up his hands. Gently, she cleaned off his face. His eyes were closed; they didn't open.

She scooped more dirt off his chest, got an arm and a shoulder under his side, and heaved so that his head and chest came free, so he could breathe. But he still didn't open his eyes. "Help me get him up!" she called. "He needs to go to a hospital."

"Ambulance is on the way," someone yelled back.

Willing hands reached down to support him while she freed his legs and feet. The dirt around her shifted and she caught her breath, but it held and they pulled him out. Then more hands reached for her.

They put him on the ground, back away from the hole, and she knelt beside him, wiping sandy soil from his face, making sure his nose and mouth were clear. "Hold on, Kenny," she whispered. "Help's coming. Just hold on."

He opened his eyes and pulled in a deep, shuddering breath.

"Good. That's good," she said. "You're awake."

"You?" He stared at her from glazed eyes.

"You're going to be all right, Kenny."

"Terry? You dug me out?"

She shrugged. "You'd have done the same for me. But good grief, Kenny, what were you doing in a hole that deep with no shoring boards?"

He coughed, spitting dirt. "Jeffries, Jeffries said not to bother. Said we didn't need . . . didn't think—" His eyelids fluttered shut.

She patted his shoulder. "Never mind. Just rest. Here comes the ambulance now."

The paramedics hurried up, and she sat back on her heels, out of their way, praying, praying that this man, this good man, would be saved.

Some minutes later, a medic turned to her. "I think he'll make it," he said. "Think you got him out in time to prevent internal injuries. Looks like

A Question of Trust   153

he's got a broken leg, though. But that'll mend. And his vital signs are good. Real good.''

She let out the breath she'd been holding. ''Thank goodness.''

He eyed her critically. ''You sure you're all right? You don't look so good.''

She managed a laugh. ''It's just dirt. I'm fine.''

But after the ambulance pulled out, siren roaring, and everyone went back to work, she stayed there, sitting in the dirt. Now that the emergency was over, she had a bad case of the shakes. How awful to be buried alive like that. Just the thought of it—

What on earth was Jeffries doing, putting Kenny to dig in a hole that deep with no shoring boards? It was downright criminal, that's what it was.

She sighed and swiped at her face with a grimy hand. Well, she couldn't sit there all day. Better get home and out of these dirty clothes. The trick would be to get past Mom without her noticing, and—

''Terry! Oh, Terry, are you hurt?''

Chapter Eighteen

She looked up. Harrison! When had he gotten there? She wanted to jump up and run into his arms, but she wasn't sure her legs would hold her. And besides, today he had the business look, and she didn't want to get dirt all over his cream-colored suit. There were workmen all around, too—she didn't want them to see her in his arms.

"No, no. I'm fine."

He glared down at her, his face a dark cloud. "You don't look fine. I saw the ambulance pulling out of here. What happened?"

"Kenny was digging a hole and the walls caved in on him. He was buried."

His face went pale. "Good grief, Terry. Is he all right?"

A Question of Trust 155

"Yes. Just a broken leg, they think."

"He's lucky. But how did *you* get so dirty?"

She didn't want to tell him. "It was nothing—really." But she could see from his expression that he didn't intend to give up until he found out what he wanted to know.

White-faced, he grabbed her hands and jerked her to her feet. But when he tried to pull her into his arms, she dug in her heels and resisted.

"Nothing?" he repeated. "You were in that hole, weren't you? You went in there to dig him out."

Why was he getting so hyper about this? She let him keep ahold of her hands, but she didn't move any closer. "Harrison, the man was buried alive. I know his wife and kids. I couldn't just leave him there to die. I had to do what I could to get him out."

"But why you?" he demanded. "Why did *you* have to do it?"

What kind of question was that? "I was there. I know what to do."

He scowled. "I told you this was no business for a woman. What if there had been another cave-in? You could have been killed!"

"But I wasn't. Harrison, for heaven's sake, calm down." She looked around, but no one was watching. Thank goodness they'd all gone back to work.

"People can get hurt anywhere. You know that. Anyway, most accidents happen at home."

"If anything ever happened to you—" He shuddered and stared deep into her eyes. "Terry, I don't think I could stand it."

She thought of her mother, the nights she'd spent crying after Dad died. What if Kenny's wife had been left to cry like that? And her so young and with little kids.

"Nothing's going to happen to me," Terry said. "Because I'm careful. But this awful accident never should have happened. It could have been prevented. Jeffries told Kenny not to bother to shore up the sides of the hole. That it would take too long. The soil was sandy and it gave way, caving in on Kenny."

She straightened her shoulders. "I'm going to the Council about this, Harrison. Jeffries should take better care of his men. There's no excuse for such carelessness."

Harrison peered at her, his forehead furrowed into a frown. "Honey?"

"Yes, what is it?"

He glanced around, his expression worried. "I wish you wouldn't do that."

"Do what?"

"Go to the Council."

She stared at him in surprise. "But why? This

A Question of Trust   157

was negligence—pure and simple. Do-It should be held responsible for it.''

''Terry, please. Just this once trust my judgment. Just this once, do what I'm telling you is right.''

Hardly believing her ears, she stared at him. ''Don't go to the Council? How can you ask me to close my eyes to such a terrible thing?''

''Can't you trust me?'' His eyes pleaded with her. ''Please?''

She pulled her hands free of his. ''Not when you want me to do something so awfully wrong. I've known Kenny Spears since kindergarten. I went to school with his wife Kathy. They have two little girls. Jeffries had no right to put him in danger like that. Just to save a few lousy dollars.''

''Terry, please. Stay out of it. Don't mess with Toohey. Let someone else—''

''Toohey!'' She glared at him. ''What's Toohey got to do with this?''

Harrison looked flustered, his face reddened, and he looked over her shoulder. ''Nothing. He's part of the Council. That's all I meant.''

But she knew that wasn't all he meant. Now she knew for sure. Harrison was Toohey's man, and Toohey and Do-It were connected to each other somehow.

Harrison leaned toward her, his expression

158 *Nina Coombs Pykare*

pleading. "Honey, I don't want you to get hurt. I love you and—"

Love? If this was love, she didn't want any part of it. "Harrison." She swallowed over the lump in her throat. "If you loved me, you'd support me, you'd want me to do the right thing. And you know what the right thing is."

"I do love you!" He glared down at her. "Though sometimes I wonder why. You're the stubbornest, most pigheaded woman I've ever known!"

"Maybe so," she said quietly. "But I do what I know is right."

"And in the process, you ruin everything!"

"What are you—" But he was already gone, stomping off as though he was the one who'd been insulted. She swallowed a sob. If he thought she'd overlook negligence like this, he didn't know her at all. Could he have been pretending to love her because he was Toohey's man? Because that's what he'd been told to do? She didn't like to think that; she didn't *want* to think that. But what had he meant—"she'd ruin everything"?

When she got home, Terry went right to her office and typed up a detailed report, citing Jeffries for his negligence. She called the messenger service to come after the report, put it in the pickup box on the porch, and went to the back door. Too

A Question of Trust 159

bad that when she'd moved in she hadn't had a connecting door made from the office into the house. It would have been easier to avoid Mom that way. But maybe if she was real quiet . . .

She opened the door and slipped into the kitchen. So far so good. Now to—

"Terry! You're home."

"Yes, Mom." Terry swung around. Maybe if she acted nonchalant, Mom would think the dirt was from the job.

Mom came through the door from the dining room, and her eyes went wide. "Terry! Whatever happened?"

"We—ah—had a little accident."

"What kind of accident?"

"Ah . . . some dirt caved in and—"

Mom let out a scream that had Tom rushing in from the living room.

"What's the matter?" he cried, looking around. "What happened?"

Mom ran into his arms. "A cave-in! Terry was in a cave-in! I knew this awful business—"

"Now, Mom. I wasn't in the cave-in. You know Kenny Spears, don't you? He works for Do-It."

Mom nodded, calmer now that Tom was holding her. "I was in PTO with his mother. Go on, tell me what happened."

"Well, Kenny was digging this hole and the walls caved in. Buried him."

160 *Nina Coombs Pykare*

She shuddered, thinking of all that dirt crushing the life from him.

"Oh my, his poor wife. And he has two babies, doesn't he?"

Terry managed a reassuring smile. "Yes, Mom. But he's okay. Well, he's going to be okay. He has a broken leg. That's all."

"Thank goodness!" Mom's forehead wrinkled in a frown. "But how did *you* get so dirty?"

Tom put an arm around her waist. "Looks pretty clear to me, honey. Terry dug him out. Ain't that right, Terry?"

"Yes."

"Oh, Terry, that's dangerous! How could you?"

Tom looked down at her. "Theresa, the man's her friend. And even if he wasn't, you want her to stand there and let the fellow die?"

Mom looked horrified. "No, of course not, but to risk—"

"She did what she had to do," Tom said firmly. "You should be real proud of her."

"I am, but . . ."

Tom laughed. "Theresa, you got to remember that Terry's a grown woman. She's not your little girl anymore. She knows what she's doing."

"But to do something so dangerous," Mom wailed. "Why can't she be more careful?"

Tom shrugged and gave Terry an apologetic

A Question of Trust 161

look. "Guess it's 'cause she's a mother," he said. "But I know she's proud of you. Me, too."

He gave her a funny look. "Harrison there, too? Did he help?"

"No, he came along after."

"Bet he was proud of you."

She shook her head. "As a matter of fact, he was even worse than Mom. Read me the riot act. Even told me not to report Jeffries's negligence. It *was* negligence, you know. The sides of that hole should have been shored up. Any fool knows that."

Tom nodded. "Don't have to be in construction to know it. Plain common sense ought to be enough."

"But why should Harrison ask you not to report it?" Mom asked, her round face screwed up in puzzlement.

"I don't know, Mom. But I didn't let it stop me. I came right home and typed out a report. The messenger service'll be picking it up any minute. The Council president should have it this afternoon."

"But Terry, won't that make trouble with that Toohey person?"

"So what?" Toohey had been nothing *but* trouble. "He won't like it. But that doesn't matter. If I don't report this, they'll keep on taking shortcuts and someone else could get killed." She straightened her shoulders. "I have to do what's right." When she had a chance to think about it, Mom would understand that.

"Of course you do," Tom said. "Thatta girl."

Blinking back tears, Terry hurried up the stairs. "Thank you, Tom," she called down to him. "That means a lot to me." It was good to have someone approve her sense of responsibility, to have someone who saw her as competent. But to have him use Dad's very words, to hear him say, "Thatta girl," that hurt while it made her feel good. Dad had always seen her that way, encouraged her in whatever she wanted to do.

Funny thing, but now that she knew him better, she could see that in certain ways Tom *was* a lot like Dad. Maybe that was why Mom loved him.

Chapter Nineteen

Two days later Terry parked her van in front of City Hall and looked at her watch. When she'd sent the Council President the report on the cave-in, she'd expected the Council to question her about it. Naturally. But something about the way Miss Ferris had summoned her to this meeting, "to answer questions about the cave-in," had made Terry feel uneasy, as though *she* was the one who'd done something wrong.

She checked her makeup in the mirror and scowled. She looked fine. What was she worrying about, anyway? She was just a citizen doing her duty. And it was time to go do it.

She got out, straightened her skirt, and headed for City Hall. Inside, she stopped for a moment to

163

164 *Nina Coombs Pykare*

put a pleasant look on her face. Then she opened the door. All seven Council members were there, sitting around the highly polished table, looking like so many solemn-faced judges with her fate in their hands. *Stop it,* she told herself. *I'm not on trial here.*

And then she saw Harrison. His face carefully blank, he occupied a chair at one end of the big table.

Her heart skipped a beat. She hadn't seen him since he'd stomped off after the cave-in. He was a stubborn, pigheaded man. There was no other way to phrase it. How could he possibly think she was wrong about this? But she wasn't going to give in—not when she knew she was right.

Though all the rest of them were looking at her, he was reading—or appearing to read—from a yellow legal pad in front of him.

"Come in, come in," Toohey ordered. "Don't just stand there in the doorway."

She stepped in and closed the door. She crossed to the table, and looked around. There was no chair for her. Toohey meant to keep her standing. He wasn't just crooked, he was also rude. She straightened her shoulders. Tom was right. She should never have gotten involved with politicians. But now that she had, she meant to do the right thing. And, after all, Toohey was only one man. There

A Question of Trust   165

were six others on the Council, six elected officials. They couldn't all be crooked. Could they?

"Now, Miss Matthews." Dr. Victor, the Council president, smiled genially. "We've called you in here to ask you some questions."

At last they were going to *do* something. "Yes, sir, I'll be glad to help the Council in any way I can."

She looked at Dr. Victor, but Toohey pointed his smelly cigar at her like a forefinger, and said, "What were you doing on the site that day?"

That was a strange question, but maybe he was leading into something else. "I went to check out some concrete we poured last week, and—"

Toohey frowned. "Do you always go back the next week to check on concrete you poured?"

Did he have to rattle off his questions like this was a third degree? A cold as the room was, she had started to sweat. "No, but it rained and—"

"You thought perhaps the job was faulty."

"No!"

"Then why this unusual behavior on your part?"

She looked around the circle. Every face was set in the same wooden lines. They might as well have been made of the missing shoring boards. No one on the Council had a bit of integrity. Or common sense either, from the looks of things.

"This job is a big one. I wanted—"

166   *Nina Coombs Pykare*

''The biggest you've ever had, isn't it?'' Toohey asked, his expression smug.

What was he getting at? Why didn't he ask about the cave-in itself? That was what she was here for—to talk about it. ''Yes, it's the biggest.''

''And you're afraid you can't handle it.''

''No. That's not true.'' She kept her voice carefully even. She'd like to wipe that cocksure grin off his face! Under her blouse the sweat was trickling down her skin. ''If I couldn't handle a job, I wouldn't bid on it.''

She risked a quick glance at Harrison, but he was studying his fingernails—the coward.

''So you made an unauthorized visit to the site,'' Toohey went on, ''and caused young Spears to—''

''I beg your pardon.'' What was the man trying to do to her? ''I did no such thing. I had every right to be on that site. And I had nothing to do with Kenny's accident, except to dig him out after it happened.''

Toohey put his pudgy fingers together in a steeple and beamed at her over them. ''So you admit it was an accident.''

''It doesn't matter what you call it. Do-It had no business putting a man in a hole like that without shoring it up and—''

''Are you an expert on digging holes?'' Toohey interrupted, his expression snide.

Please, help me. She kept a tight rein on her temper, but it took effort—a lot of effort. "It doesn't take an expert to know that that hole was dangerous."

"Then why didn't you say so before the accident?"

Careful now, don't blow it. Don't lose your cool. "I didn't look in the hole, Councilman. It wasn't part of my job. Shoring the hole was the responsibility of Jeffries, Do-It's foreman."

"But if this man Spears didn't shore it up as he was told—"

What was the matter with him? She paused and took a deep breath. Yelling wouldn't get her anywhere. "Councilman," she went on softly, "Kenny told me himself that Jeffries ordered him *not* to shore up the sides of the hole, that it took too much time."

"And we're supposed to believe your *friend*?" How could Toohey make a word sound so dirty? "Believe him instead of a respected citizen like Mr. Jeffries?"

She kept her eyes on Toohey's face. "Kenny Spears wouldn't lie about this. I know the man, and I believe him."

Toohey blew more smoke in her direction—he was deliberately trying to aggravate her. "And how *well* do you know him?" he asked.

The implication was plain. She couldn't help it,

168 *Nina Coombs Pykare*

she had to look at Harrison. For the first time he was looking directly at her, his eyes burning darkly. But still he didn't say anything. Why? Why did he just sit there like that?

And Toohey! She'd like to slap Toohey's fat red face. He was the dirtiest-minded— *Please, I need help. If I can keep my temper, maybe someone on the Council will get the message.* "Let me see. I believe Kenny and I went to kindergarten together. And his wife Kathy is a friend of mine."

"A friend. That means you'd be willing to lie for him."

He wasn't going to make her mad. She wouldn't let him. "No, sir. That's not true. I won't lie for anyone. Not anyone." She sent Harrison a hard look. "Do-It Construction was negligent in this matter. I know it. I saw it. So did a lot of others."

"Then why was yours the only complaint we received?" Dr. Victor asked.

The only one? Could Harrison have gotten to the others, stopped them somehow? "I don't know. Maybe they all knew I'd report it. But whatever anyone else says or doesn't say, I saw negligence. Gross negligence."

Toohey nodded, like some ancient brooding idol waiting to strike. But he only said, "Very well, Miss Matthews. That'll be all."

All? But there was so much more. "If you need me to testify—"

A Question of Trust   169

"That won't be necessary." Smugly he glanced around the table, and all the wooden faces looked back at him, heads nodding like so many puppets. "The Council is perfectly satisfied with Do-It's work on this contract. And we wish you would concentrate on your own business and not interfere with other—"

"Interfere? But—"

"That'll be all. Good day."

The nerve of the man! Who did he think he was?

She looked again at Harrison, but the coward had gone back to studying his hands. Her mind tumbled with words, most of them insulting, but she kept her mouth shut and with a last look at the wooden group at the table, nodded and reached for the door.

This thing wasn't going to end here. She wouldn't let it. If Toohey covered this so-called accident up, there would be proof of his dishonesty. Proof the governor would consider. She'd see to it. And not just because of today, but because it was right, because there were lives at stake.

Chapter Twenty

Closing the Council Room door behind her, Terry paused for a minute and pulled in a deep breath. What she'd like to do to that Toohey! *I know it's not up to me to do anything.* So she went out, the heels of her pumps clicking against the marble floor.

How could this happen? she asked herself, heading down the steps outside. *How could Toohey have the whole Council in his pocket?* She'd always thought the rest of them were honest men. But now—she'd never trust another politician again. She'd starve before she bid on another job in which politicians were involved.

And Harrison— He was the worst of all. Sitting there and letting that fat toad of a Toohey walk all

A Question of Trust 171

over her. Not one word in her defense. Not one! And he knew she was right! He'd even let Toohey insult her, practically call her a liar, and imply she was romantically involved with her friend's husband!

When Harrison had stomped off after the accident the other day, she'd really thought—well, at least she'd hoped—that he'd eventually come to his senses and admit she was right. But the days had passed, and hour by hour she'd come closer to admitting that she'd goofed again. It wasn't bad enough she'd chosen wrong in Jeff, now she'd been mistaken about Harrison, too.

Breaking up with Jeff had hurt a lot, but nothing like this. Jeff had betrayed her by falling for another woman, but Harrison's betrayal had been much worse. He'd wanted her to go against everything she knew was right, against her beliefs. Then he'd sat there and let Toohey drag her reputation through the mud—and never said a word in her defense, never announced that he knew it was all lies.

At the van she fumbled in her purse for the keys. Where were the darn things? She felt like she'd been run over by a truck. She just wanted to get away from here before she started to cry. A man could cuss and punch somebody, but a woman wasn't allowed that kind of outlet. Besides, she didn't believe in violence. And if she was in busi-

172   *Nina Coombs Pykare*

ness, she couldn't cry either. It was so unfair it made her want to scream. Where *were* those darn keys?

"Terry, wait. Please."

She whirled to face him. "What do you want?"

"I want to talk to you." Harrison looked around nervously.

"You mean you aren't afraid Toohey will see you talking to me? Be careful, Green, your boss will get after you!"

"Toohey's not my boss, Terry. I—" He took a step toward her.

"Get away from me!" she cried. "I hate the sight of you! You're scum, the lowest kind of scum."

"Terry, please, listen."

But nothing he could say would make any difference. Not now. Not after what had just happened. "Listen? I've listened to you long enough. Lie after lie. And all the while you've been working for that sleaze Toohey! You've got your hand in the till, too, I suppose!"

He paled and looked around again. "Terry, please, keep your voice down. You don't know what you're saying."

"That's what you think! I know, all right. And don't think I'm going to keep quiet just because you're in on it. The governor's going to hear all about this!"

A Question of Trust 173

He heaved a great sigh. "I'm sure he will, Terry. Just remember this—I love you."

Finally her frantically searching fingers found the keys. She jerked them out. "Good-bye, Harrison. Don't ever come near me again." By some miracle she got the key in the hole and unlocked the van. When she looked up again, he was walking away.

She started the motor. *Please help me make it home. I can cry when I get there.*

An hour later Terry sat at the kitchen table with her mother and Tom. "And so," she concluded, "I told him never to come near me again!"

Tom shook his head, the twinkle gone from his eyes. "Can't hardly believe it. I thought that Harrison was a straight arrow. Liked him real well."

"So did I," Terry said, with half a sob.

"Well, I *don't* believe it," Theresa said, her eyes defiant.

Tom looked at her in dismay. "Honey, didn't you hear what Terry just told us?"

"Sure, I heard. But I still don't believe it. That Harrison's a good boy. I don't believe he'd take graft. Don't believe he'd do anything dishonest, for that matter."

Terry shook her head in exasperation. Mom could be so stubborn. "Well, he did," Terry said. "All this time he's been working for that slimy

Toohey. All the while Harrison was telling me he loved me—he did tell me that, you know—he was spying on me for Toohey."

Mom shook her head. "I can't believe that, Terry. I just can't."

"Maybe your mother's right," Tom said, his voice hesitant. "She's usually pretty good about character. Hits the nail on the head 'most every time."

"Not this time." Terry pushed her chair back from the table. "And now I have to get back to work. But first"—she hugged her mom—"thanks for listening to me." She turned to Tom. "You, too." She swallowed. "And Mom, I'm glad . . . the two of you . . . found each other."

Tears came to Mom's eyes. "Thanks, honey."

Two mornings later, Terry came down to breakfast an hour late. The hot, muggy weather made sleeping hard, and she'd hardly slept a wink since the meeting with the Council anyway. Pete had said he'd take over for a few days, but inactivity was worse than facing inquisitive eyes and the whispers behind her back. In spite of everything, she had to get back to work. Work was all she had left.

She finished her toast and took a last sip of coffee. Putting this off wouldn't make it any easier.

A Question of Trust   175

"Terry!" Mom stood in the dining room doorway. "Terry, come in here and listen!"

Terry got up. "Listen to what, Mom? I've got to go to work."

"Hurry up," Tom called. "You'll miss it."

With a last look at her, Mom hurried back to Tom. Terry shrugged. She was already late. A few more minutes wouldn't matter.

"Terry?"

"Coming." She hurried into the living room and stopped cold. That was Toohey on TV—Toohey in handcuffs!

"Councilman Toohey was arrested this morning," the newsman said. "The charges are numerous. They include corruption and graft. And especially negligence in conjunction with Do-It Construction at the municipal site that almost cost a workman his life."

A picture of Kenny flashed, then the camera went briefly back to the newsman. "And here's the man responsible for Toohey's arrest—City Manager Harrison Green."

Harrison! Terry dropped into a chair, her heart in her mouth. Harrison responsible for the arrest? Harrison wasn't a crook!

She stared at his image on the screen. He looked awful, great dark circles under his eyes, his face all drawn.

"Mr. Green has been working as a special investigator, under secret orders from the governor. Tell us, Mr. Green, is it exciting to do this kind of work?''

Harrison shrugged. ''It's not glamorous or romantic, if that's what you mean. I'm no James Bond. But someone has to do it. We can't let crooks like Toohey get away with taking over our government. We have to take back our towns and cities, and make America an honest country again. I'm glad to have a part in doing that.''

''Thank you, Mr. Green.''

Mom flicked off the sound. ''Well, Terry,'' she said triumphantly. ''I hate to say it, but I told you so.''

Tom chuckled. ''One thing 'bout your mother, Terry—when she's right, she don't let you forget it.'' He winked affectionately. ''And she's right a lot.''

Terry tried to smile, but she knew it wasn't much of a smile. It was all right for Tom to make jokes about Mom. But Harrison would never forgive her for not trusting him.

She got to her feet. ''I've really got to get to work. See you later.''

Mom jumped up. ''But Terry, what about Harrison?''

''What about him, Mom? He asked me to trust him and I didn't. Harrison and I are through.''

A Question of Trust
177

Mom shook her head. "I don't believe it. Love doesn't die that easily."

"Maybe mine doesn't." She might as well admit that; they already knew it anyway. "But I've already killed his. And there's no way to bring it back."

"I suppose not," Mom said with a melodramatic sigh, that made Tom look at her suspiciously. "But I can't believe you'd be so rude."

"Rude? What're you talking about?"

"You insulted Harrison. You owe him an apology."

"Well, I suppose I did insult him. But he could have told me what he was doing."

"He was undercover," Mom said. "That means you don't tell *anyone*. Besides, you could have been working with Toohey, too. You could have been a crook."

"Mom, no way."

"But Harrison didn't know that." Mom sighed again. "And I thought I raised you to be fair."

"I *am* fair!" Terry cried in exasperation.

"Then why aren't you going to apologize to Harrison?"

"Mom, the man won't want anything to do with me now."

"You still should apologize."

Terry knew where Mom was going with this. Ever the romantic, Mom thought that bringing the two of them together would solve everything. But Terry knew better. That kind of thing only happened in the movies.

But Mom was sitting there, still waiting, her face all expectant, and finally Terry threw up her hands. "All right, all right! I'll go over after work and apologize. But it isn't going to do any good."

Chapter Twenty-one

"Terry!" Pete came hurrying up the minute she got to the municipal job, his shirt already wet with sweat. The day was going to a real scorcher. "You heard the news?"

"Yes. It was on TV."

"We heard it over the radio." Pete's honest face showed relief. "Thank goodness, they caught that Toohey. He's really a bad one." Pete sidled closer. "Did you know about it?"

She shook her head. "Nope, not a bit."

Pete's face fell. "Oh, I thought maybe that fight you told me about was a put-on. Maybe you knew what was coming down."

She sighed. "I wish I had, Pete. Maybe then I wouldn't have made such a fool of myself."

180 *Nina Coombs Pykare*

Clumsily Pete reached out to pat her shoulder. "Well, Terry, don't feel too bad. If he didn't tell you anything, how *could* you know?"

"I *should* have known," she said. "When you love someone, you're supposed to trust them—no matter what. Isn't that so?"

Pete frowned thoughtfully. "Guess that sounds good, but seems to me it could lead to a lot a trouble. What if he really *was* a crook?"

"But he wasn't. Oh, Pete! I've made such a mess of things."

Pete shrugged. "Maybe so. But I still say it can't all be your fault. Harrison made his share of mistakes, too." He looked at his watch. "We got concrete coming; better get down to work."

"Right."

If Harrison hadn't been romancing her for Toohey, then maybe he did love her. Or had loved her. After the way she'd treated him—

"Terry?"

Why was he still there? "Yes, Pete?"

"This is a hard hat area."

She stared at him. "I know that."

"Then why aren't you wearing yours?"

She glanced down in the direction of his gaze. Good grief, she was still carrying her hard hat. She clapped it on her head. "Right, Pete."

He shook his head. "Terry, I don't think you

A Question of Trust   181

ought to be here. You're—you're not thinking so straight.''

''I'll be careful, Pete. Honest.''

By mid-afternoon Terry couldn't take any more. Her heart was pounding, her mouth had gone dry, her clothes were soaking wet—and not just from the heat. If she waited till the job was done, she'd be too nervous to get a word out. She got up and picked up her knee boards and tools. She'd find Pete and tell him she was leaving.

She washed her tools and started toward the wagon to put them away. Where was Harrison likely to—

A Mercedes pulled into the lot. *His* Mercedes. She stood there, her feet stuck to the dirt, and watched it park.

She dumped the tools in the back of the van. Now there'd be no chance to take a shower before she saw him. She was such a mess, all hot and sweaty, and— But what did it matter? He was probably there to talk to Pete about something. She slammed the door shut. And what could she say to him? *I didn't love you enough. I couldn't trust you like you wanted.* How stupid.

She wanted to turn, to see where he was. And she didn't want to. Finally, she did turn. And he was there—right there in front of her.

''Hello, Terry.''

"H-hello." She couldn't tell anything from his voice, and his face was guarded. But he was wearing his cream-colored suit. She swallowed a sob. If he'd been wearing jeans and a T-shirt, she'd have known right away that he'd forgiven her. But this suit must mean—

"How are you?"

"I'm okay."

Silence grew between them. He expected her to apologize, then. And he was right—she owed him that much. Still, she wanted to hear what *he* had to say.

Finally, she couldn't stand it anymore, and the words burst from her. "Harrison, I'm sor—"

But at the same time, he said, "Terry, I'm sorry."

Then there was silence again. "I should have trusted you," she said, "but I didn't. You see, I'd heard rumors about graft. And when you came to me like you did, well, I got suspicious."

He nodded. "That's understandable. You thought I might be in with Toohey."

"Yes." She took a deep breath. "And you thought *I* might be."

He looked at her sharply. Then he sighed. "At first maybe, but not after I got to know you. I shouldn't have asked you to keep quiet about the negligence." He smiled ruefully. "I should have known you wouldn't." He shrugged. "But I was

A Question of Trust　　183

so close to getting that last piece of evidence and I was afraid you'd blow it.''

She managed a nod. ''I'm glad I didn't.''

He scowled. ''When the Council called you in and Toohey started in on you, I thought I'd explode. But I was so close to getting him, I had to keep quiet. I know you were really mad at me.''

She made a face. ''I didn't understand. I'm sorry.''

They stood there, staring at each other. He didn't move toward her; he didn't offer to touch her. Her heart fell. She'd been right. It *was* over between them. ''Well, it *was* nice of you to come and explain things,'' she said over the lump in her throat.

His eyes clouded over. ''I didn't come to explain.''

''You didn't?''

''No. I came to see how soon this job will be done.''

His eyes burned into hers and her tongue seemed to have swollen so she couldn't talk right. ''W-why?''

''You know why, Terry. You promised me your answer when this job was finished.''

She wasn't sure she heard him right. ''My . . . answer?''

He nodded. ''Surely you haven't forgotten. I asked you to marry me. And you said—''

184   *Nina Coombs Pykare*

"I know what I said. But I didn't think . . . I didn't know. . . . How can you still love—"

"I'll always love you, Terry." He looked at her, his heart in his eyes. "Always."

"Oh, Harrison, I do love you. But—but you're a special agent. How can I marry—"

And then the distance between them was gone, and she was in his arms. "Oh, Terry, you do love me."

"Yes. I said that. But—but I like my business. And how can I marry an undercover—"

He started to laugh. Clutching her against his chest, he laughed and laughed. "Honey, I'm not undercover anymore. Not with my face plastered all over TV. Besides, I'm not really an investigator."

"You're not? But the newsman said—"

"I did this for the governor. I went to school with his son. When they heard rumors about Toohey, they wanted someone they could trust. But I really am a city manager. For now, at least."

She looked up at him. "What do you mean, for now?"

He grinned. "Until you need another cement finisher."

She threw her arms around his neck. "Oh, Harrison, I love you."

"I know," he said. "Finally, I know. Say, let's

A Question of Trust 185

go tell your mother. I've got a feeling she's been waiting for this news.''

Terry laughed. ''Oh, yes, she has. And we have to tell Tom. You know, Harrison, I do like Tom. And I told them I was happy for them. You know, I want Tom to give me away.''

Harrison kissed her soundly. ''Sounds good to me.''